It's Star's last chance to prove himself in the Triple Crown . . .

The stands were overflowing with racing fans, and as the field was led onto the track for the post parade, Christina leaned forward. "They didn't give you much of a chance with forty-to-one odds, Star. Let's shock them all, okay?"

Star pranced sideways, tugging at the lead line the pony rider held. When they turned back from their warm-up gallop to go into the gate, Star loaded eagerly, dancing in place with impatience. Christina patted his neck. "Save it, boy," she murmured. "We have a mile and a half to run. You're going to need all the energy you've got to pull this off."

When the gate snapped open, Star plunged onto the track. Christina felt the colt jolt forward as his hooves hit the dirt, and she sensed herself start to pitch onto his shoulders. "Oh, no!" she gasped, struggling to keep her balance. "This isn't happening!"

Collect all the books in the Thoroughbred series

Collect all the books in the Ashleigh series

*coming soon

THOROUGHBRED

STAR'S INSPIRATION

CREATED BY

JOANNA CAMPBELL

WRITTEN BY

MARY ANDERSON

HarperEntertainment

An Imprint of HarperCollinsPublishers

■ HarperEntertainment

An Imprint of HarperCollins*Publishers*

10 East 53rd Street, New York, NY 10022-5299

This is a work of fiction. The characters, incidents, and dialogues are
products of the author's imagination and are not to be construed
as real. Any resemblance to actual events or persons, living
or dead, is entirely coincidental.

▦ Produced by 17th Street Productions,
an Alloy Online, Inc., company

HarperCollins books are available at special quantity discounts for bulk
purchases for sales promotions, premiums, or fund-raising.
For information please call or write:
Special Markets Department, HarperCollins Publishers Inc.,
10 East 53rd Street, New York, NY 10022-5299.
Telephone: (212) 207-7528. Fax: (212) 207-7222.

ISBN 0-06-009051-0

HarperCollins®, ■®, and HarperEntertainment™
are trademarks of HarperCollins Publishers Inc.

Cover art © 2003 by 17th Street Productions,
an Alloy Online, Inc., company

First printing: June 2003

Printed in the United States of America

Visit HarperEntertainment on the World Wide Web at
www.harpercollins.com

❖ 10 9 8 7 6 5 4 3 2 1

STAR'S INSPIRATION

1

CHRISTINA REESE CROUCHED OVER WONDER'S STAR'S
shoulders, staring between the colt's alert ears at the
Belmont racetrack. She could see the marks where the
track crew had raked the surface, leaving shallow
grooves that stretched away from the gate, eventually
blending together in the distance. The curve in the
oval of the track looked as though it were miles away.
Christina squinted through her goggles, reassuring
herself that the racetrack was all right. Her eyes were
playing tricks on her.

"We'll be okay," she murmured to Star. Beneath
her, the chestnut Thoroughbred shifted his weight.
The colt was so wound up that Christina could feel his
tension humming through the reins she gripped

tightly. "I know we'll be fine," she whispered, trying to reassure herself as much as Star.

To their left, in the number four chute of the starting gate, Christina could hear the snorted breaths of the Celtic Meadows horse, Wild 'n' Free. His jockey, Justin Powers, spoke quietly to the horse, trying to soothe him. A grandson of the Triple Crown winner Affirmed, the colt was a throwback to his grandsire. The striking resemblance to Affirmed had drawn a lot of media attention to Wild 'n' Free before the Preakness. The colt, trained in Ireland, had placed second in the race.

To Christina's right, she could hear the thud of hoofbeats as Townsend Acres' Celtic Mist danced in place. Emilio Casados, Celtic Mist's jockey, murmured in Spanish to the colt. Although Christina couldn't tell what Emilio was saying, she could tell by his tone of voice that he was trying to calm the agitated horse. Celtic Mist shared bloodlines with Wild 'n' Free and had been bred at the same farm. The powerful gray colt had placed second in the Kentucky Derby and had won the Preakness.

Christina was painfully aware of the threat that Celtic Mist and Wild 'n' Free could pose on the track. She knew both horses were strong distance runners, but she tried not to think about the pressure they would put on Star during the one-and-a-half-mile race. She needed to concentrate on getting her colt through the longest, most important race of his life.

"The Belmont," she said to the colt, still awestruck by the idea that they were riding in the oldest of the Triple Crown races. "We're racing in the Belmont, Star."

A shudder ran through the colt, and Christina felt it echo through her own taut muscles. Star had run in the Kentucky Derby and lost; in the Preakness he had placed third by default after the jockey riding Gratis for Tall Oaks had been disqualified.

"We'll be just fine," she repeated to Star. Suddenly aware of a moment of complete stillness, she braced herself for the start, perched over Star's shoulders, her helmet strapped tight and her goggles firmly in place. She didn't carry a crop, knowing that she didn't need it to communicate with Star. She had a special bond with the colt that made her feel as though she were a part of him when they were running. Star seemed to know what she was thinking, and that was a big part of their success on the track.

Christina didn't hear the starting bell, but suddenly the gate was open and Star was plunging forward. The track seemed to fall away beneath him, and Christina felt herself hurtling into space, the track footing rushing up to meet her. She automatically ducked her shoulder, preparing for the impact. But her thoughts were on Star and what had caused him to collapse. Her mind was crowded with flashes of the end of the Kentucky Derby, when her cousin Melanie's filly, Perfect Image, had gone down with a broken leg at the end of the race. She thought of Star lying on the track, his front leg shattered, and she cried out in horror.

"Christina, wake up!"

Ashleigh Griffen's voice broke Christina's fall. She sat up with a jerk, gasping for air. Her mother stood beside her bed, looking at her with a worried frown, and for a moment Christina couldn't figure out why Ashleigh was standing on the track and why it was so dark. She shook her head, struggling with the idea that she wasn't at Belmont Park. It took her a minute to realize she was at Whitebrook, her parents' Thoroughbred farm in Lexington, Kentucky, safe in her own bed.

"I heard you call out," Ashleigh said, sweeping a hand through her tangled hair as she sat down on the edge of Christina's bed. "You sounded so upset. That must have been one terrible nightmare you were having."

4

Christina dragged her hands across her face and exhaled heavily, still trying to clear the tattered fragments of her dream from her mind. That was all it had been, a horrible dream. "I'm okay now, Mom," she said, forcing a weak smile. "Thanks for waking me up." Star was in the barn, she reminded herself, sleeping in his stall.

"You're sure you're all right?" Ashleigh asked, resting a hand on Christina's shoulder. "What was the nightmare about?"

Christina shook her head. "I really don't remember," she said, not wanting to share the terrible image of Star breaking down right out of the starting gate.

"Okay," Ashleigh said reluctantly. She rose, tugging at the belt of her flannel robe. "I'm going back to bed." She glanced at the clock on Christina's nightstand. "It's only two o'clock. Can you go back to sleep?"

Christina shrugged. "I'm going to go downstairs and get a glass of milk," she said. Christina felt bad about waking her mother. Ashleigh, and Christina's father, Mike Reese, worked long hours on the farm. They didn't need to be getting up in the middle of the night to check on Christina as though she were eight instead of eighteen.

"A glass of milk sounds like a good idea," Ashleigh agreed. "I'll see you a little closer to dawn, all right?"

"Thanks, Mom," Christina said, rising as Ashleigh left the room. She listened to her mother's footsteps, then the sound of her parents' bedroom door closing. Christina quickly slipped into a pair of jeans and a sweatshirt, then padded down to the kitchen in her bare feet. Instead of going to the refrigerator, she tugged on barn boots from the assorted pairs sitting by the door and slipped outside, pulling the door closed quietly.

The Reeses' old white farmhouse sat on a knoll overlooking the sprawling fields and long barns that housed Whitebrook's Thoroughbreds, and Christina paused on the porch to gaze at the moonlit scene. The early June moon was almost full, casting a white light over the farm. The moonlight seemed to wash the color from everything, leaving only the starkness of dark and light. Even the path down to the barns looked like nothing more than a dark ribbon meandering down the hill. Christina stepped from the porch and followed the trail down to the barn where the racehorses were kept.

She reminded herself again that the terrible scene at the Belmont racetrack had just been a nightmare, but the whole awful thing had seemed so real that she needed to see for herself that Star was all right.

The vapor lights around Whitebrook's barns gave off a cold glow, enhancing the moon's shadows, draining even more color from the farm's grounds. Christina hurried into the barn, pausing at the doorway while her eyes adjusted to the gloom. The interior of the barn was softly lit by several small bulbs along the aisle, and Christina could see the dark shapes of the Thoroughbreds in their stalls. As they sensed her presence, several of the horses lifted their heads and greeted her. In the stall nearest the door, four-year-old Rascal shifted and nickered, and Christina paused to give the horse's neck a pet.

"Go back to sleep," she told him. "You still have hours before you have to get up. I'll be quiet, I promise." She walked the length of the aisle until she neared Star's stall. As she approached, the colt raised his head and snuffled at the air, then emitted a soft grunt as he caught her scent.

"It's me, boy," Christina said, letting herself into his stall. Even in the dimly lit barn Star's chestnut coat glistened, thanks to frequent groomings and a good diet. Christina ran her hand along his sleek neck as the colt nuzzled her jacket, searching the pockets for treats. It was still hard to imagine that Star had been deathly ill the previous winter. No one had ever thought he would recover to become a Triple Crown contender.

"I didn't bring you anything," she murmured, gently rubbing the base of his ear. When Star didn't find any hidden goodies, he snorted quietly and nudged her chest.

"I just needed to be sure you were okay," Christina told the racehorse, wrapping her arms around his neck. She buried her face in his mane and inhaled deeply, taking in Star's sweet, familiar fragrance. "You're just fine, aren't you?" she murmured, giving him a squeeze.

The three-year-old colt bobbed his head, and Christina chuckled. "I take it you didn't have the same nightmare I did," she said, leaning down to run her hand along Star's long, slender legs. "You were probably sleeping perfectly well until I disturbed you."

Feeling the strength in Star's legs helped reassure Christina that her dream had been just that and nothing more. "I'm going to sit here with you for a while," she told the colt. "Just until you go back to sleep, all right?" She sat down in the deep bedding that lined Star's stall and leaned her back against the wall. Star stood over her, blowing warm air into her hair, and

Christina reached up to rub his velvety soft nose.

Now that she knew Star was fine, the nagging fear that had come with the nightmare faded. She felt a little silly for rushing down to the barn in the middle of the night. As the tension that had kept her feeling wide awake began to fade, her eyes grew heavy. "Just a few more minutes," she told Star. "Then I need to get back to bed."

Star's rhythmic breathing soothed her, and soon her eyelids dropped. She tried to force herself to open them, but it took too much effort. She started to raise her hand to rub her eyes, but her limbs felt as though they were set in concrete. As she drifted back to sleep, her last thought was that Star's stall was a very comfortable place to be.

"Do you want some milk and a spoon with your pan of grain?"

Dani Martens's voice startled Christina, who snapped her head up, banging it against the hard wall of the stall. "Ouch!" she exclaimed, reaching up to rub the back of her head. She twisted her neck, giving the groom a baleful look.

Dani was leaning over Star's stall door, grinning down at Christina. "We could fix you up with your

9

very own stall, you know," she said, laughing. "I don't think Star should have to share his space with you. He might start charging you room and board."

Christina scrambled to her feet, dusting bedding from her jeans. "What time is it?" she asked, gently pushing Star's nose away as the colt tried to nibble on her tousled hair.

"Almost five o'clock," Dani said, hooking a full net of hay inside the stall. "You and Star looked so peaceful—you curled up in the corner and him with his nose in your hair—I didn't want to disturb you. In fact," she said, "I should have dug out my camera. That would have been a great photo for the front page of the *Racing Times*. Couldn't you just see the caption?" She gestured as though she were holding up a newspaper. "'Jockey and Horse in Late-Night Conference to Discuss Winning Belmont Strategies.'"

Christina yawned and stretched, trying to work the kinks out of her stiff muscles. "Thanks for letting me sleep," Christina said. "And thanks for not taking a picture. I'm sure I would have looked really great with my mouth hanging open and hay stuck in my hair."

Dani nodded. "You do look like you could use a shower."

"That'll have to wait," Christina said with a groan. "I have a lot to get done this morning."

Dani shook her head as she poured a can of grain into Star's feed pan. "You're not working Star this morning, right?" she asked. "I already told Ian and Maureen that I would help exercise some of the other horses, and I have time to clean a few extra stalls." Dani smiled. "You were really out cold," she said. "I figured if you ended up in Star's stall for the night, you must have been pretty restless, so I thought I'd give you a little extra time to catch some sleep."

Star turned from Christina to tug a mouthful of hay from the net, and Christina let herself out of the stall, pulling some bits of hay from her hair. "I don't want to make you work extra just because of me," she said.

Dani grinned at Christina. "I'll be working full-time through the summer," she said. "I won't go back to short hours until college starts back up in the fall. With Melanie staying at Townsend Acres until Image gets better, Ian and your mom agreed that they need the extra help around here. I need the money for school, so it works out great for me."

Christina's cousin, Melanie Graham, was living at Townsend Acres, the Thoroughbred farm owned by the parents of Christina's friend Parker Townsend. After the racehorse Melanie trained and jockeyed, Perfect Image, had broken her leg during the Kentucky Derby the previous month, the Townsends had offered

11

Image's owner, the rock musician Jazz Taylor, the use of their therapy pool and equine medical facility to aid in Image's recovery. As Image's trainer and jockey, Melanie had stayed at Townsend Acres to work with the vets treating the filly.

"Well, thanks for covering for me," Christina said. "I appreciate it."

"It isn't a problem," Dani replied.

"I'd better get up to the house and shower," Christina said, looking down at her disheveled clothing. "We have graduation practice today. I don't think I'd be too popular with the rest of my classmates if I showed up looking and smelling like I spent the night in the barn."

"Have fun," Dani said, grabbing the handles of the wheelbarrow she had loaded with hay nets and cans of grain. "I'll get the chores taken care of."

Christina hurried from the barn, eager to get out of her grubby clothes and into a nice hot shower. But when she got outside, Parker Townsend was climbing from the cab of his pickup. Christina rubbed her eyes, wondering what had brought Parker by so early.

Christina wondered if she still had hay in her hair, and was a little surprised by her concern about her appearance. She had thought she was beyond caring

12

about what Parker thought of her, but she knew deep down that he was more important to her than she wanted to admit.

Ever since she had started racing seriously the previous year, and Parker had begun to pursue his goal of being on the United States Equestrian Team, they had drifted apart. Even now, he was only in Kentucky temporarily. He was supposed to be in England for the summer, training with Jack Dalton, one of Britain's premier eventing instructors. But Parker's grandfather had surprised him by buying him a ticket home to attend the Triple Crown. Christina felt her cheeks redden at the thought that, more than anything, Parker had probably come home to support her. Conveniently, he'd been around to take her to the prom—though she'd been so stressed out about preparing for the races, neither one of them had had a great time. Still, Parker's presence must mean that she was still very important to him. *He's important to me, too*, Christina thought as Parker spotted her and grinned. She smiled and waved back. Parker strode across the yard, looking well rested and alert, dressed in a tidy polo shirt, jeans, and polished paddock boots. His dark hair was cut close, his jaw freshly shaved. Christina sighed to herself. As usual, Parker looked great, and she knew it didn't matter that they were moving in different directions. She still had feelings for Parker that rekindled every time she saw him.

Parker looked down at her, then raised his eyebrows. As he started to open his mouth, Christina raised her hand to silence him.

"Don't say a word," she said. "I know I look like I spent the night in a barn."

"I was just going to say good morning," Parker said mildly. "But now that you mention it, you do look a little more rumpled than usual." He reached out and plucked something from Christina's hair, frowning thoughtfully. "It looks like timothy hay to me," he said. "Do you think changing your diet to horse feed is going to help you run faster in the Belmont? I hate to burst your bubble, but Star is the one who has to run. You shouldn't be walking off with his food like that."

"Funny," Christina said, scowling at Parker as she raked her fingers through her hair, catching more bits of hay under her nails. "What are you doing here?"

When Parker's face turned serious, Christina felt her stomach drop a little. "I'm worried about Melanie."

"What's going on?" Christina asked.

"Mel is so wrapped up in Image's recovery that she

doesn't realize how much my dad is manipulating her," Parker said.

"What's Brad doing now?" Christina asked, sighing heavily. It seemed as if Brad Townsend was always up to something. She knew her cousin had been so distraught over Image's injuries that she hadn't stopped to question why Brad was willing to help with the filly's recovery. But Christina had had her own experiences with Brad when the Townsends had co-owned Star, and she knew he never did anything out of kindness. The only reason Brad had given up his interest in Star was because he thought the colt was going to die.

"I heard Dad talking to the vet who's taking care of Image," Parker said. "He's keeping track of the cost of having Image at Townsend Acres, right down to the last penny. He's had a couple of long talks with the farm's breeding manager and with Ralph Dunkirk, the head trainer. From what I can tell, I'm pretty sure Dad is working on a plan to breed Image to Celtic Mist and retain full ownership of the first live foal."

"He can't do that!" Christina exclaimed.

"He can if he convinces Melanie that it's a fair trade," Parker said dryly.

"Jazz wouldn't let it happen," Christina said quickly. Jazz was far more worldly than Melanie when it came to dealing with unscrupulous characters such as Brad.

Parker shrugged. "If Dad gets Melanie on his side, Melanie will be able to get Jazz to agree. Dad can be pretty ruthless. You know that, Chris."

Christina sighed and nodded. "So what are we going to do to stop him?" she asked. Her mind was swimming with all the things she had going on. She and Melanie were graduating from high school next week, and days later she was riding Wonder's Star in the Belmont Stakes, the third leg of the Triple Crown series. She felt overwhelmed already by just finishing school and racing in the Belmont, but now she had to help protect her cousin from Brad Townsend's connivances. As if Melanie would appreciate her interfering anyway.

The two had barely spoken in the last few months. Before the Kentucky Derby, Melanie had moved Perfect Image to Townsend Acres because of the security available at the Townsends'. The strain on Christina and Melanie's relationship had been hard on both girls, and since Brad had taken Melanie and Image in before the Kentucky Derby, Melanie seemed more and more distant from the Reeses. Christina was worried about her cousin, but there wasn't a lot she could do.

"I'll keep an eye on things at home," Parker promised. "I'm not there much, but I'll do what I can."

"I'll try to talk to Mel at school today," Christina said. She heaved another deep sigh. "Not that it will do a lot of good."

"Things still aren't okay between you two, huh?" Parker asked. "I thought maybe if Mel was staying around Townsend Acres for a while, she'd miss how much more pleasant things are here."

Christina gave an indifferent shrug. "She's got it pretty good at your folks' place," she said. "The guest cottage is nicer than our house. But maybe Dad or Mom could talk to Will, and he could get through to her." Melanie's father, Will Graham, was a record producer in New York who was supportive of Melanie's passion for Thoroughbred racing but not very knowledgeable about the business.

"It's worth a shot," Parker agreed. He glanced at his watch and frowned. "I have to get over to Whisperwood," he said. "I'm covering lessons for Sammy today. She and Tor had an appointment in Lexington, so I'd better get going."

Christina gazed up at Parker. She wanted to tell him how much she missed him, but the words died on her lips as he gave her a quick wave and turned away.

"See you," he called over his shoulder as he headed for his truck.

"Yeah," Christina muttered as he drove away. "See you." Parker had stopped by only because of what was going on with Melanie. He obviously didn't have time to spend with her, and she would do well not to let seeing him once in a while get her hopes up.

She dragged her fingers through her hair again, trying to shake the feeling of disappointment that had settled over her. She gave up on her hair and headed for the house and her long-overdue shower.

2

CHRISTINA SLIPPED INTO THE HIGH SCHOOL AUDITORIUM and scanned the large room, looking for a place to sit. She saw Melanie and Katie Garrity sitting together, an empty chair beside them. *Good*, Christina thought, starting in that direction. This would give her a chance to talk to both of the other girls.

Ever since the senior prom two weeks before, Katie hadn't had much to say to her. Christina had been so immersed in Triple Crown preparations that she had neglected her friends, and she really didn't want to graduate without making amends. But as she headed for the row, another senior, Allen Smith, walked over and sat down next to Katie. Christina sighed. So much for spending a little time with Melanie and Katie. She found another empty chair and settled onto it.

The day dragged by. The principal, the school counselors, and some of the teachers spent time talking to the senior class, and then the students practiced walking up to the stage, where they would be handed their diplomas. Christina thought she was going to die of boredom. She squirmed in her seat, trying to pay attention to what was going on.

"Considering that we're going to be heading out to face the real world in a few days, I think it's a little late for them to teach us how to walk," the girl sitting next to Christina muttered as a nervous student tripped walking up the stairs.

The dry comment made Christina smile, and she nodded in agreement. Finally practice ended, and with a sigh of relief she left the auditorium, her thoughts on getting back to Whitebrook and spending time with Star. The weather was perfect for a short hack on the trails behind the farm. But as she left the building, Christina realized she still hadn't talked to Melanie, and a conversation with her cousin was long overdue.

She stood outside the auditorium, her back pressed against the cinder-block wall, gazing around at the campus while she waited for Melanie and Katie to walk outside. In just a few days they'd be done with school. She envied Melanie a little. Her cousin had never expressed any interest in furthering her education. She had been focused on a future in racing from the time she had moved to Whitebrook at the age of twelve.

Christina hadn't been quite so clear. Just a few weeks ago she had been completely tired of studying, sure she wanted to get away from books and learning, but now she was wondering about her own future.

Horse racing was her greatest passion, but the more she thought about it, Star had been her biggest reason for starting to race. The connection she had with the colt seemed almost magical. When she was riding him, she felt as though they were one creature. But as a three-year-old, Star had only a couple more years of racing left before he was retired to stud. Would she be as eager to race once Star was done on the track?

A group of her classmates came out of the auditorium, discussing their plans after graduation.

"I can hardly believe that the next time I walk into a classroom, it'll be at the University of Kentucky," a tall blond girl was saying as she walked by Christina.

"I know," the boy next to her said. "It's going to be weird to leave here for Michigan at the end of summer."

"I kind of wish I was leaving the state to go to college," another girl said. "But I'm stuck with going to the community college."

"There are worse things to do than go to the community college," someone retorted.

"I know," she replied with a sigh. "My parents have told me that maybe after a couple of years there I'll have a better idea what I want to do."

After a few more minutes, Melanie and Katie still hadn't come outside, so finally Christina shoved away from the wall, walking slowly to where she had parked the Blazer. She felt isolated from the rest of her class, and it was her own doing. She climbed into the Blazer, wondering if Melanie missed driving it. She and Melanie had bought the four-wheel-drive together, but while Melanie was staying at Townsend Acres, Brad had loaned her a car.

No wonder Melanie was so taken with the Townsends, Christina thought as she drove away from the high school. Brad was really going out of his way to make sure she and Image had everything they needed. How could she ever convince Melanie that Brad wasn't acting out of kindness, that there would be a price to pay for whatever she accepted?

As she turned onto the road and headed for White-brook, Christina found herself thinking about college again. "Maybe it isn't too late to try to register at the university for fall classes," she murmured to herself. Or maybe the community college would be a good idea.

Or maybe, she reminded herself, all she needed was to work with horses. She had put a lot of money away with Star's win in the Louisiana Derby. Buying a place of her own and starting a breeding farm with Star at stud wouldn't be the worst move in the world. The fact that the Kentucky Derby–winning mare Ash-leigh's Wonder was his dam, along with Star's having overcome great obstacles to succeed on the track, would make him a good draw as a stud.

When she reached Whitebrook, Christina parked near the house and changed into a pair of jeans, then pulled on a pair of boots before she went down to the barn. As she walked by her mother's office, she could hear Ashleigh in a one-sided conversation. She stepped inside the door to see her mother sitting at her desk, the phone cradled between her ear and shoulder. Ashleigh smiled at Christina, then gestured at one of the folding chairs across from her desk. Christina moved a pile of back issues of the *Daily Racing Form* and sat down, waiting for Ashleigh to finish her phone call.

"Great," Ashleigh said, nodding at what the person on the other end of the line was saying. "We'll be there on Saturday morning. Thanks so much for the invitation. I'm looking forward to seeing you."

Christina waited impatiently for her mother to end the call, curious as to what was going on.

Finally Ashleigh hung up the phone and turned her attention to Christina. "That was Ghyllian Hollis," she said. "She's invited us to visit Celtic Meadows."

"Cool," Christina said. "I'd like to see some of her other horses." Christina had been awed by the ability Ghyllian's colt Wild 'n' Free had shown on the track. The Irish-trained Thoroughbred had placed second in the Preakness two weeks earlier. Vince Jones, a trainer Christina had ridden for several times, was now working for Ghyllian, and Christina was eager to see what other racing prospects Vince was training for Celtic Meadows.

"Maybe Melanie would like to go with us," Ashleigh suggested. "I know you two haven't done much together since things got so strained before the Derby,

24

but since she's been helping the Townsends with Celtic Mist, she might be interested in meeting the colt's breeder."

Christina nodded thoughtfully. "That a great idea," she said, happy that her mother might have just given her a good way to reconnect with her cousin. "I'll call her."

But when Christina dialed the number to the Townsend Acres guest cottage, she got Melanie's answering machine. Disappointed, she left a message and hung up, then left her mother's office, stopping to pick up a lead line and halter before going out to Star's paddock. When she reached the gate, she leaned her arms on the top of the white rail fence and gazed at her colt for a minute.

Star's copper-colored coat gleamed. His silky tail hung in a glistening red-gold cascade, brushing below his hocks as he dozed in the warmth of the afternoon sun. Christina sighed. Star was still the most important thing in the world to her. She had spent the last three years dedicating herself to him, and she had to admit that her efforts had been well worthwhile.

She had a connection with Star that she'd never experienced with any of the other horses she'd been around. Not even Sterling Dream, the gray jumper she had sold to Tor and Samantha Nelson, who owned Whisperwood, the farm where Parker worked and usually kept his horses, Ozzie and Foxy. Samantha's father, Ian McLean, was Whitebrook's head trainer. Samantha's sister, Cindy McLean, was a retired jockey who now worked for Tall Oaks as Gratis's trainer.

Christina made a soft clucking noise, and Star raised his head to look at her. When she looked into his dark, intelligent eyes, she knew that Star would do anything for her. With a soft whinny, he started across the paddock, his attention fixed on Christina.

She opened the gate and lifted the halter to slip it over his sleek nose. Star shoved his head forward and she clipped the halter in place, then took him into the barn to groom him. In a few minutes she had the colt saddled. She did a quick check of his leg wraps and then started to lead him outside.

"Hey, do you want some company?" Dani was walking down the aisle, holding an armful of freshly oiled tack.

"That would be great," Christina said. "Do you want to saddle Rascal and take him out?"

"I'll have him ready in a minute," Dani said, hurrying toward the tack room with her bundle.

Christina led Star to a mounting block near the

barn door and swung onto his back. Star snorted softly and tossed his head, then pawed the ground impatiently as Christina adjusted her stirrups.

She warmed the colt up by walking him in slow circles for a few minutes. Star was so responsive to her, it took little effort to communicate what she wanted him to do. "We make a great team, don't we, boy?" she asked, leaning forward to massage his poll with her fingertips. Star craned his graceful neck, lipping at the toe of her boot, and Christina smiled to herself as she stroked his neck.

"Just think," she said. "In another week we'll be in New York, getting ready to ride in the Belmont." Star bobbed his head as if he knew what she was saying.

"It'll be a lot different from when we were there last winter," Christina said, running her hand down the colt's muscular shoulder. It was hard to believe that Star had been so ill just six months earlier that the vets had suggested putting him down.

The fact that he had recovered to race in the Triple Crown was something Christina hadn't ever dreamed possible. But when they lost the Derby, her disappointment had been overwhelming, and it had been difficult for her to put her priorities back into perspective. Their third-place finish in the Preakness had helped her remember that Star was the main reason she loved to race. Now she knew that just getting to ride her own racehorse in the Belmont was good enough, and placing in the race would only be a bonus.

"We're ready to go," Dani said, leading Rascal out of the barn and swinging into the saddle. In a minute the girls were jogging the horses along the wide tractor lane that ran between the paddocks, and soon they were cantering along the well-groomed paths that wound through the woods bordering the farm.

"This is so much fun," Dani said, perched lightly on Rascal's back. "I love riding as much as I love working with the horses."

Christina nodded, keeping her weight low on Star's back so he wouldn't get the idea that they were racing. "Did you always know you wanted to become a veterinarian?" she asked Dani. The young groom was starting her third year of college, with plans to earn a degree in veterinary medicine.

Dani slowed Rascal to a trot. "No," she said. "I always thought I'd be a circus performer."

Christina gave the other girl a startled look. "You're kidding, right?" she said.

"Oh, no," Dani said seriously. "I wanted to wear those sparkly costumes and gallop around doing stunts on a big white horse."

Christina bit down a snort of laughter at the idea of Dani standing on her head on a galloping circus horse. "Uh . . . what changed your mind?" she asked, focusing her gaze between Star's alert ears.

"I started learning to do some trick riding," Dani said. "It's lots of hard work, you know."

Christina sobered a little and looked at Dani's serious expression.

"When we had an injured horse and the vet asked me to give him a hand," Dani continued, "I realized that if I became a veterinarian, I could spend as much time with animals as I wanted *and* do something that could help them. And not just horses," she added. "I love taking care of all kinds of animals."

"It sounds like it was a pretty easy choice," Christina said, thinking about her own future. She didn't like the idea that the rest of her life was a vast unknown.

"I was so glad to get out of high school that I never thought I'd go to college," Dani admitted. "But once I started taking classes at the community college I was able to appreciate what the teachers were offering me."

They rode on in silence, Christina turning over in her mind the things Dani had said. By the time they rode back to the barn, Christina was still struggling with the choices she had to make. She untacked Star and groomed him thoroughly while Dani took care of Rascal, then finished her chores.

"If I was a vet, I could take care of you better if you ever got sick again," Christina murmured to Star as she put him in his stall. "But it takes years of school. Do I want to do that?"

Star nuzzled her, and Christina gave the white whorl on his forehead a rub with her fingertips. "No matter what I do," she promised the colt, "I'll always be here for you."

On Saturday morning, when Ashleigh turned the car onto the drive that led to Celtic Meadows' grounds, Christina stared out the window, trying to take in the entire view at once. Beside her, Melanie let out a soft whistle. Christina glanced at her cousin and grinned. Melanie's eyes were riveted on a field next to the driveway. Half a dozen yearlings were turned out in the large pasture, and as Christina looked from horse to horse, each one appeared more impressive than the last. Even though they were young, she could see the quality of the breeding in each of the colts. Long legs, strong shoulders, graceful necks, perfectly formed heads—every one of Ghyllian Hollis's yearling crop looked like a potential winner.

"Those guys look awesome," Melanie murmured.

Christina nodded. "They look like a Kentucky Derby field waiting to happen, don't they?" she agreed. She thought about Celtic Mist, Brad Townsend's Thoroughbred, who had won the Preakness. The racehorse had come from Celtic Meadows, but to Christina, any of the colts they were looking at right now was at least as impressive as Brad Townsend's colt. Ghyllian Hollis had money to invest in her breeding program, and her attention to quality showed in every one of her young horses.

Christina turned her head as Ashleigh slowed the car near a long barn. The building was painted kelly green with white trim, decorated with a band of Irish knotwork. "There's Ghyllian," Ashleigh said, nodding toward the open doorway. "Vince is with her."

As the Reeses and Melanie climbed from the car, the trainer raised his hand in greeting.

"Welcome to Celtic Meadows," Ghyllian said with a friendly smile. "Vince and I were just discussing Wild 'n' Free's training for the Belmont."

"You have some great horses here," Melanie said. "How come we haven't seen your horses at the track before the Preakness?"

"I've been working with horses in Ireland," Ghyllian said. "My father preferred his native country to the United States, so we kept our main facility in Shannon. Dad's real passion was steeplechasing. He was breeding more for that type of race than flat track, although he always wanted to have a horse that could make it into the Triple Crown. When he passed on a few years ago, I began bringing American Thoroughbreds to Ireland to see if I could make his dream come true.

"Unfortunately we didn't get things together in time to compete in the Derby." She glanced at Vince and smiled. "But thanks to Vince's hard work, Wild 'n' Free made a pretty decent showing in the Preakness."

"Second place?" Melanie asked, shaking her head. "That's more than decent. Your colt did an amazing job."

"We were pretty pleased," Vince said, looking at Melanie. "How's your filly doing?" he asked. "I've heard great things about Brad Townsend's therapy pool."

"You should come over and see Image," Melanie replied. "She's doing so well that even the vets are thinking she won't need much more water work." Regular work in the equine therapy pool at Townsend Acres had given Image the exercise she needed without putting any stress on her broken leg, keeping the filly from being trapped in a stall and sling. "That pool is the only thing that saved her," Melanie said. "I really owe Brad a lot."

Christina cringed at Melanie's words. Parker hadn't been exaggerating when he said Melanie was going to get herself into a difficult situation with Brad.

"I was just heading over to look at some of the two-year-olds we're starting to race," Vince said. "Do you want to see some of Celtic Meadows' up-and-coming racehorses?"

"Yes," Christina and Melanie exclaimed at the same time.

"I'd really like to see the stallion barn first," Ashleigh said, looking at Ghyllian. "If you don't mind, that is."

"Let me take you on a tour," Ghyllian replied. "We can catch up with Vince and the girls later." She and Ashleigh left Christina and Melanie with Vince and headed into the barn.

"This way, ladies," the trainer said, gesturing at a golf cart parked near the barn. "I'm used to ambling around the shed rows at the track, not hiking across five-acre paddocks."

When Christina and Melanie started to laugh, Vince scowled at them. "I'm not getting any younger, you know. Hop on and hang on." He climbed behind the wheel of the little cart, and Christina and Melanie clung to the sides, laughing as Vince drove the length of the barn and toward another sprawling green building.

"We could have walked faster than he's driving," Melanie said, looking across the top of the cart at Christina.

Christina smiled back. She was glad Melanie had agreed to come to the farm with them. At least they were having a little fun together, and that was a start. She still needed to figure out how to bring up the subject of Brad and Image, but it definitely wasn't the right time. When they reached a wide tractor lane running between rows of white-fenced paddocks, Vince slowed to a stop and the girls hopped off the cart.

"Look at him," Melanie said, pointing at a handsome bay colt who was eyeing the cart with intense curiosity.

"He's a half brother to Wild 'n' Free," Vince said. "Ghyllian named him Celtic Knot. Can you believe the quality of horses we have here? I was seriously planning to retire until Ghyllian asked me to work with Wild 'n' Free. It was too great a chance to turn down."

"No kidding," Christina said, walking to the fence

as the colt crossed the paddock. "So he's got Affirmed bloodlines, just like Wild 'n' Free?"

Vince nodded. "He's had three starts and won two," he said. "We have him entered to race on Thursday at Churchill Downs." He looked from Christina to Melanie. "Would either of you be interested in racing him for us?"

Christina started to open her mouth to accept the offer, but from the corner of her eye she saw Melanie's expression, and she released her breath without saying anything. Instead she looked at Melanie, giving her cousin a chance to take Vince up on the opportunity to ride the colt.

"I'd love to," Melanie said slowly. "But Ralph Dunkirk, Brad's trainer, asked me to ride for Townsend Acres. I don't know which races they want me for."

"Oh," was all Christina could say.

"I couldn't exactly tell him no," Melanie said defensively, tightening her jaw as she looked at Christina.

"It's great to hear you're able to ride again," Vince interjected. "I was glad to see you back in the saddle after that broken rib from your tumble in the Derby had you sidelined. You seem to have bounced back quite nicely." He turned to Christina. "How about you? Would you like to race for Celtic Meadows?"

"Of course," Christina said, then turned to Melanie and forced a smile. "Maybe we'll be racing against each other."

Melanie shrugged neutrally. "Maybe," she said.

Christina turned her attention back to the colt, reaching out to stroke his neck. So much for talking to Melanie about Brad, she thought. There was no way she could bring the subject up without Melanie getting defensive, and Christina knew she couldn't talk about Brad without expressing her intense dislike for the man.

As they toured the rest of the paddocks and admired Celtic Meadows' horses, Melanie stayed quiet, and by the time they met up with Ashleigh and Ghyllian, Christina felt as though a dark cloud had settled over her. Were she and Melanie ever going to be friends again? It didn't seem right that they had become so close since Melanie had moved to Whitebrook, only to have things fall apart now.

"ISN'T THAT BEN'S FRIEND, DEL ABDULLAH?" ASHLEIGH asked as she led Charisma between the shed rows of Churchill Downs on Thursday morning. Ben al-Rihani, the owner of Tall Oaks, had introduced the Reeses to Del at a party a few weeks earlier. A businessman from Dubai, Del owned Magnifique, a last-minute entry in the Belmont.

Charisma, one of Whitebrook's two-year-old fillies, snorted loudly, darting looks left and right as she took in the strange place. Ashleigh patted her glossy red-gold shoulder as she gazed at the tall dark-haired man standing in the aisle between the shed rows.

Mike looked in the direction Ashleigh was pointing and nodded. "That's him," he said. "I wonder if he's got another horse besides Magnifique that he's racing today."

Christina remembered the powerful bay colt, who had been at Pimlico during the week before Preakness. Christina had seen the colt work on the Maryland track, and she knew he was going to be tough competition for the rest of the field in the Belmont.

When they got closer, Del looked in their direction and smiled brightly, then strode across the wide aisle to meet them. "Mike Reese and Ashleigh Griffen," he said, extending his hand. "It is good to see you again." He nodded to Christina. "Are you riding this filly today, Christina?" he asked, eyeing Charisma closely. "She is a fine-looking Thoroughbred."

"This is Charisma," Christina said, stroking the filly's nose. Charisma snorted again and tossed her head, tense with excitement. Ashleigh gave the lead line a tug, and the filly danced her hindquarters sideways, clearly eager to keep moving.

"Ben told me Whitebrook has excellent stock," Del said admiringly. "He was absolutely right. I am impressed." He laughed. "I am quite new to Thoroughbred racing," he admitted. "But I am learning quickly to recognize quality breeding when I see it."

"Do you have a horse running today?" Ashleigh asked.

Del shook his head. "Magnifique is the only race-horse I own," he admitted. "After Ben introduced me to Wonder's Champion when the stallion was in Dubai, and I saw some of the foals they were producing, I couldn't resist buying a horse of my own."

When Ben's father had bought Champion years before, he had moved the horse to the United Arab Emirates, and had only recently returned the stallion to the United States to stand stud at Tall Oaks. As business partners, Ben and Cindy now co-owned the Triple Crown–winning Thoroughbred.

Del grinned at Ashleigh. "I even tried to buy Champion from Ben's father, but Sheik al-Rihani wouldn't sell that horse for any amount of money."

"Champion hasn't raced in fourteen years," Ashleigh commented.

"But he is such a majestic animal," Del said. "The first time I saw him, I knew I had to have a horse like that, whether he was young enough to race or not."

"But you've got Magnifique," Christina said. "He's awesome, and boy, can he run!"

Del nodded in agreement. "I was fortunate to have an agent in Kentucky with a good eye for quality. Magnifique has some excellent bloodlines, with Seattle Slew on both the top and bottom," he said, referring to the colt's breeding on both the sire's and dam's sides.

"Really?" Ashleigh said, sounding impressed. "My parents had a Seattle Slew mare." She smiled at the memory. "Slewette was a great dam. She gave us some wonderful foals." Her expression fell a little. "We had some great years at Edgardale when I was young." She released a heavy sigh.

Christina was certain her mother was remembering the terrible year when a virus had forced the Griffens into losing Edgardale, their Kentucky breeding farm. She knew her mother must be thinking about the horses they had lost because of the epidemic.

"We'd better get Charisma to her stall," Mike broke in. "We need to get her ready to race."

"It was good to see you again," Del said, then looked at Christina. "I look forward to seeing you ride." He smiled. "Today, that is. Next week at Belmont I won't be as happy to see you on Wonder's Star. You and that colt of yours are going to give Magnifique a run for his money."

"Thank you," Christina said, pleased with the compliment. "I was just thinking the same thing about your colt."

When they reached Whitebrook's designated stall, Christina busied herself grooming Charisma before she went in search of Vince Jones to discuss the race she was to ride for Celtic Meadows.

40

She found Vince in the track kitchen, eating a hearty breakfast of pancakes and sausage.

"Have a seat," he told Christina when she walked up to the table. "Would you like a bite to eat?"

Christina shook her head. "After I race," she said. "I don't want to be overweight for my first race for Celtic Meadows."

Vince chuckled, then took another bite of sausage. "You look like you'll need to throw some extra weight on your saddle anyway," he said. He patted his stomach. "I never could have been a jockey. I like my food too much."

"Is that why you became a trainer?" Christina asked.

Vince nodded. "That's it," he said. "I can eat like a horse and let you littler people do all the hard work."

After they discussed Vince's strategy for Christina's race, she returned to Charisma's stall, slowing when she saw Brad Townsend standing near the stall talking to Mike. She glanced around to see if Melanie was around, but her cousin was nowhere in sight. Christina thought about heading for the jockeys' lounge to avoid being around Brad. Maybe Melanie was there. She started to turn in that direction but then stopped. She was not going to let Brad intimidate her. She squared her shoulders and strode up to Charisma's stall.

"I hear Image is healing nicely," she heard Mike say to Brad when she was within earshot.

"Thanks to my facility," Brad said, giving Christina a brief, cool nod. "Jazz and Melanie are lucky that I was able to accommodate their filly."

"Image is a real fighter, too," Christina broke in, irritated that Brad seemed to be taking all the credit for Image's recovery. "She's got a lot of spirit, and that makes all the difference in the world."

Brad shrugged. "Her recovery is primarily because of the team of experts I hired to work with her," he said, turning his attention back to Mike. "We've been working Celtic Mist in the therapy pool, too," he added. "The water work has really enhanced his strength. I expect that the Belmont won't be much of a challenge for him. My colt is more than ready for the race."

Christina stiffened, clenching her jaw tightly. Her father gave her a quick look and with an almost imperceptible shake of his head warned her to keep her mouth shut.

"I'm heading for the jockeys' lounge," she said through tight lips, knowing that if she stood and listened to Brad for another minute, she wouldn't be able to keep quiet.

"We'll see you at the viewing paddock before the fourth race," Mike said.

Christina walked away, seething inwardly at Brad's arrogance. By the time she reached the jockeys' dressing rooms, she had cooled down a little. She didn't see Melanie in the main lounge, and she went into the women's dressing room, dropping her bag on a bench in front of a row of lockers.

"Hey, Reese," a familiar voice called out.

Christina looked up to see Vicky Frontiere tucking her brightly colored racing shirt into the white breeches she was wearing. Vicky, an old friend of Ashleigh's, had helped Christina get her jockey's license the previous year. She had ridden TV Time in the Kentucky Derby and the Preakness. Although the colt had put in a poor performance in both races, his owner was paying Vicky generously to ride him in the Belmont as well, because the publicity was good for her television company.

"Hi, Vicky," Christina said, sitting down on the bench. She yanked her shoes off and started to dig into her bag for her breeches.

"You look a little tense," Vicky commented. "Is everything okay?"

Christina glanced up and nodded. "I'm fine," she said tersely.

"Then you'd better relax that jaw of yours before you break some teeth," Vicky replied in a teasing voice.

Christina gave the other jockey a baleful look. "You spend a minute or two listening to Brad Townsend talk and then tell me that," she said.

Vicky rolled her eyes. "I just turned down two rides on Townsend Acres horses," she said. "I'd rather not be associated with Brad and his crew. They have some fine Thoroughbreds, but there isn't a purse in the world big enough to tempt me to ride for that man."

Christina felt slightly better knowing that Brad affected other people the same way he affected her. She relaxed a little as she smiled at Vicky.

"That's better," Vicky said, grinning back as she picked up her helmet and racing saddle. "I need to weigh in and head for the track. I'm riding in the first and third races."

"Good luck," Christina said. "I have horses in the fourth and sixth races today."

"Well, then," Vicky said, pausing before she walked out the door, "I'll wish you luck, too, as long as we're not racing each other."

"That'll be next week," Christina said. "I'll be breaking out of the gate with you at Belmont." Vicky let the door shut behind her, and Christina dressed in her silks, then pulled her tall boots on. She went to have her weight checked. Each rider had to make the same weight in order to make sure none of the horses had the advantage of an underweight rider. If that happened, weights would be placed into pockets in the horse's saddle blanket. Once the clerk at the scale had confirmed that with her saddle in hand Christina was at weight, she settled onto an easy chair to watch the races on the TV in the lounge.

As soon as the third race had begun, Christina headed for the viewing paddock, where her parents were waiting with Charisma.

"Keep it light," Ashleigh reminded Christina when she settled onto Charisma's back. "It would be nice if she won, but I don't expect her to win her first race."

"Got it," Christina said, adjusting her stirrups as Dani led the prancing chestnut filly to the track.

They had the number five position in the starting gate, and Christina crouched over Charisma's neck, settling into place while the last two fillies were being loaded into their chutes. When the gate opened, Charisma hesitated for a moment before leaping onto the track, and Christina urged her toward the rail, several strides behind the rest of the field.

"Take it easy," she told the filly, but Charisma was determined to pass the leader, and Christina gave up trying to keep her slow. The Whitebrook filly felt strong and steady, and Christina relaxed a little, set-tling onto the saddle so that the excited racehorse could run, all the while careful not to allow her to over-stress herself.

"Attagirl," Christina said, smiling when Charisma flicked her ears back in response to her rider's voice. "You're doing great." Charisma dug her hooves into the ground and stretched her legs, easily passing the first three horses.

"You run like a colt," Christina said admiringly, easing her hands up the filly's muscular neck. Soon they were beside the lead filly, and Christina leaned forward slightly. "You can do this," she said, feeling the filly strain against the hold Christina had on the reins. Charisma pushed her nose out, lengthened her strides, and as they crossed the finish line of the seven-furlong race, Charisma was in first place.

"Great job!" Ashleigh exclaimed when she met them on the track as Christina brought Charisma back toward the starting gate. The filly pranced and tossed her head as Ashleigh caught the reins.

Christina vaulted to the ground, grinning broadly. "She was awesome," she told her mother. "We could have kept going for another mile, I'm sure! Maybe she'll be our next entry in the Triple Crown. Think about it," she said. "Another Whitebrook filly winning the Kentucky Derby. Wouldn't that be great?"

"We'll see how things go next year," Ashleigh said, leading Charisma to the winner's circle. "Let's get a few more races under her girth before we nominate her for entry in the Derby."

Christina pulled the saddle from the filly's sweat-soaked back and slung it over her arm while she weighed in with the clerk of the scales. After a brief ceremony in the winner's circle, she headed back to the locker room to change into Celtic Meadows' silks, emerald green emblazoned with a silver harp, while Ashleigh took Charisma to the veterinarian barn for the drug testing required of the first three horses in every race.

While Christina was tucking Celtic Meadows' silks into her breeches, someone came into the locker room. She looked up to see her cousin standing near the door.

"You rode a good race," Melanie said, offering Christina a hint of a smile.

"Thanks," Christina replied, smoothing her hands down the front of her shirt. "Charisma was awesome on the track. She's fun to ride."

"Good luck on Celtic Knot," Melanie added, sounding a little wistful. "I think he's going to be a rocket on the track."

"I hope so," Christina said. "It would be great to

have two wins today. How did you do for the Townsends?" she asked, happy that she and Melanie were able to talk a little. "I missed your ride in the first race."

"I brought my colt in second," Melanie said.

"Are you riding again?" Christina asked. "I didn't see your name on the program."

"Brad named me to ride in the seventh race," Melanie said, looking at Christina's shirt. "I wouldn't mind riding for Celtic Meadows," she added.

"You could have ridden Celtic Knot," Christina reminded her.

Melanie glanced down at the green-and-gold Townsend Acres silks she was wearing, then looked back up. "I told Brad I'd make sure I was available for any races he wanted," she said. "Considering how much he's done for Image, I couldn't do any less."

Christina nodded in understanding. "How much longer will Image be at Townsend Acres?"

A shadow crossed Melanie's face, and she shrugged. "It depends on what Brad's vets say," she said. "I don't want to push Image's recovery."

Christina had a nagging feeling that Melanie wasn't telling her everything, but it seemed that when she mentioned Brad or Townsend Acres, Melanie shut her out. How was she supposed to give Melanie a warning about Brad when it felt as though she was walking on eggshells every time they talked?

"Are you ready for tomorrow night?" Christina asked, eager to find something else to talk about. "Can you believe we're really going to graduate?"

Melanie's smile seemed a little more relaxed. "My dad says getting me through high school has been like pushing a boulder uphill," she said with a small chuckle. "I'll be glad when I have that diploma in my hand, so I know I'm really and truly done."

"Me too," Christina said. She glanced at the clock on the wall and gasped. "I'd better get out to the track," she said. "I'll be cheering for you when you race."

"Thanks," Melanie replied. "I'll be yelling for you, too."

Christina walked rapidly back out to the viewing paddock, where Ghyllian Hollis was waiting for her.

"Good luck out there," the Celtic Meadows owner said. "I'd give you some last-minute advice, but I know you've already gone over the race with Vince, so I'll keep my mouth shut and not tell you how to do your job."

"I'll do my best for you," Christina promised.

When the groom brought Celtic Knot around, Christina vaulted lightly onto the colt's back and headed for the waiting pony horses.

Celtic Knot seemed eager to run as soon as he set foot on the track. The pony rider kept him in check, and Christina watched the other colts in the field during the post parade, quickly measuring up the competition.

When they were closed into the gate, she patted Celtic Knot's mahogany neck. "We'll have to watch out for that chestnut in chute number two," she told the colt. "He looks like a ball of fire." Celtic Knot snorted and tossed his head, and Christina laughed. "I know," she said as though the colt had spoken to her. "He may be a ball of fire, but you're a turbocharged rocket, right?"

When the starting bell rang, Celtic Knot dove onto the track with such force that Christina had to catch his mane to keep her balance. The poles marking the furlongs for the half-mile race shot past them, and as they crossed the finish line Celtic Knot was in a photo finish with the chestnut colt Christina had been concerned about. When the tote board flashed the finish order, Christina was disappointed to see that her colt had come in second.

Vince Jones met her as she left the track after handing Celtic Knot off to his handler.

"You did great," the trainer said, clapping his hand onto her shoulder. "I didn't think Celtic Knot could keep up with that chestnut. That other colt has already set some impressive records."

"So you're okay with second place?" Christina asked. "I was a little disappointed."

Vince shook his head firmly. "I'd like you to ride more often for us," he said. "I used to watch your mother race, and you have the same light touch that Ashleigh did. You bring out the best in the horses you ride, Chris."

Christina smiled hesitantly. "I was thinking about limiting my racing and taking some college classes this fall," she said.

Vince frowned at her. "Are you kidding? College will always be there, but you're in top condition now. It would be a waste of your talents not to get all the racing in that you can while you're young and strong."

"I don't know," Christina said slowly.

"Look at the money you made just today," Vince reminded her. "The jockey's purses for those two races would pay for quite a few classes. Ride now, put your money away, and let college wait until later."

Before Christina could think of a response, Melanie's race was being announced. Vince walked away, and Christina turned to the track, moving to the rail to watch her cousin ride for Townsend Acres.

She found a discarded program, curious as to which Townsend Acres horse Melanie was racing. The colt, a bay called Halfmoon, had four starts with no wins on his record. Of the other two-year-olds in the race, three already had several wins to their credit. Christina frowned thoughtfully as she reviewed the program. Was Brad trying to set Melanie up to fail?

When the race started, Christina stood rigid, her hands gripping the rail tensely. "Go, Mel," she called, her eyes glued on the green-and-gold Townsend Acres silks as the closely packed horses surged out of the starting gate. When they came around the curve of the track, she realized she was holding her breath, her muscles as taut as though she were running the race herself.

Melanie's mount was in the middle of the field, and it didn't look as though she would be able to make a move before the race ended. But when a gap appeared between the two front-runners, Christina watched her cousin rise a little higher in her stirrups and swing her hand back to tap Halfmoon's hip with her crop.

The colt plunged into the gap, and as they crossed

the finish line Melanie was solidly in second place. Christina cheered loudly, impressed with the skillful way Melanie had maneuvered the colt into a good position.

When Melanie walked back toward the backside after turning the colt over to his groom, Christina smiled and waved at her. "Good job, Mel!" she called.

Melanie glanced up and darted a smile at her, but as she veered in Christina's direction Brad stepped up to the rail and gestured at her. Christina glanced over at him and felt her stomach tense.

"That was some solid riding," Brad said to Melanie, smiling broadly as she reached the rail. "If you keep racing like that, I'll always have rides for you."

Melanie's face lit up as she stopped in front of Brad. "Halfmoon did a great job for me," she said happily. "Thanks for letting me ride him."

"Just think of what we could do with a foal by Celtic Mist out of Image," Brad said. "We'd have a horse with the best combination of bloodlines ever. Affirmed, Seattle Slew, and Alydar on both top and bottom. Imagine it, Melanie."

Christina recoiled at his words and waited for Melanie to snap a quick "forget that" at Brad. But instead Melanie gave Brad a thoughtful look and nodded.

"That might be one incredible foal," she agreed. "We'll have to talk to Jazz about it."

Christina felt her jaw sag. She watched Melanie continue down the track toward the locker rooms, and realized she needed to go change out of her silks as well. She hurried after her cousin, trying to figure out what she could say that would make Melanie aware of what Brad was doing—putting her in a situation where she was obligated to him, and using that to take advantage of her and Jazz.

But by the time Christina reached the lockers, Melanie was already in the shower, and several other jockeys came in before Christina could say anything to Melanie. With the room full of people she wasn't about to get into a discussion about Brad Townsend with her cousin.

Christina chewed at her lower lip while she was changing her clothes, unable to figure out a way to get through to Melanie. Brad was clearly using his oily charm to ensnare her cousin, not because he cared about Melanie and her racing career but because, even if he couldn't have Image, he had found a way to own at least part of her offspring.

Christina groaned to herself. It seemed almost like the deal Clay Townsend had worked out with Ashleigh over Wonder's foals years before. But Clay

Townsend had been generous in giving Ashleigh half ownership of Wonder and her foals out of his gratitude for the work she had done with Wonder. When Clay had handed control of Townsend Acres over to his son, Brad had made the situation almost impossible. Why couldn't Melanie see what Brad was up to now?

4

ASHLEIGH WAS JUST COMING IN THE MAIN DOOR TO THE jockeys' lounge when Christina came out of the locker room. "We need to get home," Ashleigh said. "Ian just called. The vet is on his way." She turned on her heel and headed for the door. "Your father has Charisma loaded and he's waiting for us."

"What's wrong?" Christina demanded, hurrying after her mother as Ashleigh strode outside and began walking toward the back gate at a rapid pace.

"Star," her mother replied without slowing down. "Ian said there's something wrong with Star."

A jolt of horror raced through Christina and she lengthened her strides, passing her mother as they neared the gate. "What is it?" she asked, fighting down the urge to bolt for the truck.

"Ian wasn't sure," Ashleigh said. "He just said Star didn't seem right, and he'd called Dr. Seymour."

Mike had the truck running, and Christina scrambled into the cab after Ashleigh, buckling her seat belt as her father drove out of the lot. She kept her hands tightly clenched, feeling her panic increase as the miles crept by.

The two-hour drive to Lexington seemed to take an eternity. Christina knew her father was driving as fast as was safe, especially pulling the horse trailer behind them, but she had her foot pressed to the truck's floorboard as though it were the gas pedal, willing them to cover the distance at a higher speed.

Ashleigh reached over and patted her knee. "It'll be okay, Chris," she said. "I'm sure everything is fine." But the tension in her voice kept her words from sounding convincing.

Christina swallowed hard, her eyes fixed on the road in front of them. "Thanks, Mom," she said. "But I won't know that until I've seen Star."

"I know," Ashleigh said, falling silent. They drove the rest of the way to Whitebrook without speaking. When they finally reached the farm, Christina dove from the truck before her father had completely stopped in front of the barn. She dashed inside and ran to Star's stall, her mind full of images of the colt lying down, paralyzed the way he had been last winter. Dr. John Seymour was standing in front of the stall with Ian, putting his stethoscope back into his bag. Christina's heart lurched. Had the vet given up already?

"What's wrong with him?" Christina demanded as she got close, her voice cracking with fear. Before the vet could answer, Christina saw Star. The colt was standing in his stall, looking at her, his eyes clear and bright. A wave of relief swept over her, and when he nickered low in his throat she slipped into the stall and threw her arms around him.

"You're all right," she said, burying her face in his warm neck. The colt nudged her and grunted quietly. Christina looked at the vet. "What was wrong?" she asked again. "Is the virus coming back?"

Dr. Seymour offered her a reassuring smile. "I'm sure it's nothing," he said. "Ian was concerned because Star was off his feed this morning and seemed a little lackluster during the day. Rather than take a chance, he called me."

Ian nodded. "I figured it was better to be safe than sorry," he told Christina. "I didn't mean to alarm you, but I did want you to know what was going on."

"I recommend you keep a close eye on Star," Dr. Seymour said as Mike and Ashleigh hurried up to the stall. "We'll try a change in his feed, and I suggest a couple days of layoff before you take him up to Belmont. We don't want him too stressed." He gazed thoughtfully at Star. "The Triple Crown race schedule is hard enough on the horses. Star needs to be pampered more than the average racehorse because of his recent medical problems."

Ashleigh nodded. "Having him take it easy for a couple of days is a good idea," she agreed. "He's been doing really well, so we don't need to push him."

Christina sighed softly and hugged Star's neck. "You'd better stay okay," she murmured to the colt, who wrapped his neck around her, resting his chin on her shoulder in a horsy hug.

"If he isn't eating the way you think he should, or if he isn't acting perfectly normal, call me tomorrow," Dr. Seymour said, picking up his bag.

After the vet left, Christina stayed with Star, afraid that if she left for even a few minutes, he would be down when she returned. She knew she was being a little superstitious, but she stuck beside the colt anyway. Nothing mattered to her as much as Star's well-being. She prepared his feed herself and watched closely while he ate, relieved to see that his appetite seemed quite healthy. After watching over him for several hours, Christina reluctantly left the stall.

It was still dark the next morning when Christina hurried down to the barn. Star whinnied eagerly when she approached his stall, a can of feed in her hands. When she filled his grain pan and put it down for him, the colt plunged his nose into it, greedily devouring the grain and supplements.

Christina smiled, overjoyed. "You're fine, aren't you?" she asked the colt, stroking his sleek shoulder while he ate. "What happened yesterday? Were you jealous that I was off racing other horses while you were home with nothing to do?" She knew Star loved to run more than anything, but as Dr. Seymour had said, the stress of the Triple Crown schedule was hard on the Thoroughbreds under the best of conditions. Star's medical history made it even more important to be extra careful with him.

She left him to finish his breakfast and headed for the track so that she could help Ian and Maureen Mack, his assistant, work with the two-year-olds. As she walked past Ashleigh's office her mother gestured to her. "Cindy just called," Ashleigh said. "Can you run over to Tall Oaks this morning? She needs someone to exercise Gratis for her, and you and Melanie are the only two people she could get on short notice who can handle the colt."

"What about Wolf?" Christina asked.

Ashleigh rolled her eyes. "Apparently after he was suspended for his illegal riding in the Preakness, Wolf has quit working for Tall Oaks."

Christina nodded. She liked the young rider, but Wolf had a cocky attitude and was an aggressive rider. His riding had gotten him into trouble during the second Triple Crown race. Even though he had brought Gratis in in third place, because of his riding Gratis had been disqualified. As a result, Star had been credited with placing third in the race.

"What about the work I have to do here?" Christina asked.

"Dani can help Ian and Maureen this morning," Ashleigh said. "I've already got it worked out if you'll go help Cindy."

"Of course I'll go," Christina said. "Cindy and Ben must be in a panic trying to find a jockey for the Belmont."

Ashleigh nodded. "They sure are," she said. "I remember what they went through before they put

Wolf on him. I don't know what they're going to do now." She glanced at the calendar hanging on her wall. "Just don't dawdle," she added. "You still have graduation tonight."

Christina stared wide-eyed at her mother. "I completely forgot!" she said, shaking her head, then laughed at herself. "Maybe deep down I don't want to leave high school."

"Maybe you have so much going on right now that you can't deal with what's going to happen beyond the Belmont," Ashleigh replied.

"Maybe that's it," Christina said.

"You're under a lot of pressure right now," Ashleigh said, leaning back in her chair. "I do understand, you know. Let's just get through next week, and then we can talk about your long-range plans."

"Okay," Christina said, grateful for her mother's understanding. "I'll be home in plenty of time to get ready for tonight," she promised.

When she reached Tall Oaks, Cindy already had Gratis at the practice track, saddled and ready to ride. Christina pulled her helmet on and buckled it into place as she walked from the Blazer to the track.

"Thanks for doing this for me," Cindy said, flicking Gratis in the nose when he tried to nip her. "I don't know what I'm going to do for a jockey now that Wolf is banned from racing."

"What about Melanie?" Christina asked. "Maybe she could ride for you." Maybe naming Melanie on Gratis would help pull her cousin away from Brad's influence, while giving Ben and Cindy a jockey who could handle their difficult colt. High-strung and temperamental, Gratis had always been a challenge to ride. Christina had worked with the colt during the winter, grateful for the chance to prove to Vince Jones and several other trainers that she was a solid jockey.

Gratis had been worth the effort. He was well bred, fast, and strong, and Christina had succeeded with him when more seasoned jockeys had failed with the colt. The experience had helped give Christina a reputation as a jockey who could handle any kind of horse, and she had been offered more rides than she could accept because of it.

Cindy raised her eyebrows. "I thought Melanie was committed to riding for Townsend Acres," she said.

Christina shrugged. "You'd have to ask her," she replied. "But she won't be riding Celtic Mist in the Belmont, and Brad doesn't exactly own her."

Cindy gazed thoughtfully at Gratis, then looked at

Christina, a smile slowly spreading across her face. "That's a great idea," she said. "While you're warming Gratis up, I'll go call her." She gave Christina a boost onto Gratis's back, waiting by the rail while Christina rode the colt onto the track.

As soon as Christina had him moving, the colt tried to bolt with her. She moved him in a tight circle, keeping a firm grip on the reins. After a minute she felt him relax a little. Straightening him, she rode close to the outside rail, prepared for any new stunts Gratis might pull. She thought of the times the colt had dumped her on the track.

"You're not going to get away with anything, buster," she said firmly, tightening her grip on the reins. He went smoothly for several strides, then tried a small buck, but Christina could tell his heart wasn't in it. As he humped his back, she gave him a quick rap on the hip with her crop. Immediately Gratis brought his head forward and gave it a quick shake, then settled into a steady trot, moving along the rail as though he had never thought about giving his rider a difficult time.

After their first circuit of the track, Christina gave Cindy a thumbs-up. Cindy nodded, then turned away from the track, heading for her office.

Christina focused her attention on working Gratis, and by the time Cindy returned to the track, the colt was warm and eager to move out.

"He looks great," Cindy called as Christina rode past her. "You can open him up a bit. One lap at a hand gallop, please."

Christina cued Gratis into a gallop and settled into the rhythm of the colt's steady gait, as impressed with his powerful strides as she had been the first time she rode the colt. "You are one awesome racehorse," she told the big bay as they galloped easily along the rail. Gratis seemed to get stronger as they continued around the track, and Christina exhaled heavily as she realized that with Melanie in control of the colt, Gratis stood a good chance of sweeping the field in the Belmont. What had she been thinking to increase the odds against Star?

By the time she was done with Gratis, worry had settled a heavy weight on Christina's shoulders. Tall Oaks' fiery bay colt seemed to be right at the top of his game, and with Wild 'n' Free, Celtic Mist, and Magnifique running in the Belmont, the fierce competition might be more than Star could handle. Maybe she was expecting too much of her colt.

Riddled with doubt about racing Star in the last leg

of the Triple Crown, she brought Gratis to a stop near where Cindy was standing at the rail. As she dismounted, she saw a car pull to a stop near the barn. Melanie climbed from the driver's seat.

Beckie, Gratis's groom, walked up to the track from the barn. Christina handed her the colt's lead and patted his sweaty shoulder. "He worked hard," she told the Australian groom. "He really needs a good cooling out."

"I'll take care of him," Beckie said without her usual perky smile.

"Are you all right?" Christina asked. She enjoyed Beckie, who was always cheerful and enthusiastic. For the groom to be acting so down was completely out of character.

Beckie gave a little shrug. "I kind of miss having Wolf around," she admitted. "When he ruined the Preakness for Tall Oaks, he and Cindy got in a big argument, and he left without a word to anyone."

"That was pretty rude of him," Christina said. She knew Beckie liked the jockey, and she thought Wolf was a jerk to walk away with saying a word to the groom.

Beckie looked at Christina, a little of the familiar twinkle in her eyes. "It's all right," she said. "If he acts like that, I wouldn't want to waste my time on him anyway."

"Good for you," Christina said, pleased to see that Beckie wasn't going to mope around over Wolf. She gave Gratis's rump a pat as Beckie led the colt away to walk him out.

By the time she reached Cindy and Melanie, the pair were deep in conversation. Melanie gave her a quick smile, then turned back to Cindy.

"Celtic Mist is really looking solid for the race," Melanie said to the Tall Oaks trainer. "Brad and I are talking about breeding him to Image next spring. With her win in the Derby, and Celtic Mist's win in the Preakness, and possibly the Belmont, those bloodlines are too good not to combine."

Christina bit down on the inside of her cheek. That didn't sound like Melanie talking. She was sure her cousin was parroting Brad's words. But she smiled at Melanie. "Are you ready for tonight?" she asked.

Melanie nodded firmly. "Graduation at long last," she said with a happy sigh.

"Is Jazz going to be here for the ceremony?" Christina asked.

Melanie's expression dropped a little. "No," she said. "But he sent me a dozen roses and a card, so I know he's thinking of me. Once I'm done with school, I'll be free to do some traveling, so maybe I can see some of his concerts in Europe. That, and I can focus on racing. I can hardly wait."

"How would you like to focus on racing in the Belmont?" Cindy asked.

Melanie gave her a quizzical look. "Emilio Casados is riding Celtic Mist," she said. "Brad told me if something happens that they need a new jockey, he'd keep me in mind, but I know there are other jockeys he'd ask first."

"How about riding for Tall Oaks?" Cindy asked. "I've seen you on Gratis, and Ben and I would love to have you race for us."

Melanie's eyes went wide and a broad smile stretched across her face. "Do you mean that?" she gasped.

"Absolutely." Cindy nodded, her expression serious. "Will you do it?"

"Of course!" Melanie exclaimed, flinging her arms around Cindy in an enthusiastic hug. She whirled to face Christina. "I'm riding in the Belmont!" she said, her voice filled with disbelief. "Is that the most incredible thing? Everything is going right for me!"

Her joy was infectious, and Christina couldn't help

but be pleased at how happy Melanie was, no matter what kind of pressure it put on her and Star.

"I'm glad," she said sincerely, fighting down the worries that nagged at her about Star's condition and the stress she was under. She knew Melanie had been devastated by Image's breakdown in the Derby. If racing Gratis in the Belmont helped her cousin get past that, and helped her refocus her direction on racing and not on what Brad wanted, it was a good thing.

"I need to get back to Townsend Acres," Melanie said. "Image goes into the therapy pool in half an hour, and I want to be there to help with her exercise."

"How is she doing?" Cindy asked. "Do they plan to keep working her in the water much longer?"

"I haven't talked much to the vets," Melanie admitted. "They work for Brad, so most of my information comes from him. But she seems to be doing really well. They're talking about light ground work, just walking on a lead, and only on soft ground, in a week or so." She pursed her lips. "I'm still afraid something is going to go wrong and she'll reinjure herself, so I'm okay with them being cautious about her progress."

"Will you be here tomorrow to start working Gratis?" Cindy asked.

"I'll be here first thing," Melanie said. She glanced

at Christina. "I'll see you at graduation tonight, okay?"

Christina nodded, pretending to flip the tassel on her mortarboard from side to side. "Right to left, or left to right?" she joked.

"Either way, we'll be done with high school tonight," Melanie said. "See you later."

After Melanie left, Cindy turned to Christina, a grim look on her face. "I wonder if Brad is being straight with her," she said.

Christina nodded. "I was thinking the same thing," she said. "But I think Melanie doesn't want to question him too much. After all, if it weren't for Townsend Acres and Brad, Image wouldn't have survived."

"I'm a little concerned about what kind of game Brad's playing," Cindy said.

"Parker is worried, too," Christina told her. "But I can't talk to Melanie about it. She just gets defensive."

"I'll mention it to Ben," Cindy said. "We can give Jazz a call, and maybe he can find a way to check up on Brad and get more information from the vets as to how Image is doing without putting Melanie in a position where she's challenging Brad. She's got a fine line to walk with him right now."

Christina nodded. "I need to get home," she said. "I still have chores to do."

"Thanks so much for coming over," Cindy said. "I really appreciate it. You must be pretty excited about graduating," she added with a grin.

Christina shrugged. "I was," she said. "But now I'm a little torn. I didn't spend much time thinking about anything beyond getting done with high school, but now I have decisions to make, and it's harder than I thought."

"I know you've heard it all before," Cindy said. "But keep in mind that you shouldn't rely on being able to jockey and train. Getting a college degree now would take some pressure off you if you can't ride." She tilted her head toward her bad shoulder. "I've been very lucky," she said. "I want to see you do well, too, and not just bank on luck."

"Thanks, Cindy. I'll talk to you later."

Christina drove home, her mind spinning with thoughts of the upcoming Belmont, Vince Jones's advice on putting her energy into racing now and letting the future take care of itself, and Cindy's thoughts about attending college.

"I don't even know what I'd study," she said out loud, taking in the rolling pastures of the farms that lined the road. Cindy was taking business classes, Parker was getting a business degree, and Dani was studying to be a vet. What would she do if she went to college? Maybe instead of narrowing her focus on getting good grades, she should have thought more about the information she was getting out of her high school classes. *It's a little late now,* she admonished herself. *You graduate tonight, Reese. You can't go back, so it's time to move forward.* But as she pulled into Whitebrook's driveway she couldn't imagine what she would be doing in the future. She promised herself that as soon as the Belmont was over she'd dig out the college catalogs that she'd set aside and see if there was a direction she could focus on. There had to be something she could do that involved horses, but she wasn't quite sure what it might be.

5

WHEN CHRISTINA GOT HOME, SHE WENT STRAIGHT TO THE barn to check on Star. Dani had already moved the colt to his turnout, and Christina stood at the fence admiring the way the sun made his red-gold coat glisten. He moved gracefully across the paddock, looking so magnificent and powerful that Christina couldn't tear her gaze from him. It hardly seemed real that he was her very own.

She rested her forearms on the fence rail and sighed. As worried as she was about the Belmont next week, she knew Star had to race. He had been born to run, and in spite of all the setbacks they had encountered, he was at his best right now.

Star walked over to the fence and shoved his nose at her, demanding a pet. "You look perfect," she told the colt, scratching his poll. "I have to get to work now," she said. "Enjoy your leisure time."

She spent the rest of the morning helping the trainers work on ground-training the yearlings, graduation forgotten.

"Shouldn't you be getting ready to go?" Ian finally asked.

"Go where?" Christina gave him a puzzled look, then remembered. She slapped her forehead with the palm of her hand and laughed. "Never mind! I'll see you later." She rushed to the house so that she could shower and change.

By the time she came down the stairs wearing a new dress Ashleigh had bought her for graduation, her graduation gown over her arm, she was a bundle of nerves. She stood in the living room and looked uncertainly at her father. Ashleigh had driven to the Blue Grass Airport near Keeneland to pick up Will and Susan Graham, who were flying down to see Melanie graduate.

"Relax," Mike told her, crossing the room to give her a hug. "It isn't the end of high school, honey. It's the beginning of the rest of your life."

Christina tried to smile at him but failed. "I'll be fine," she said. "I need to get over to the school, so I'll see you there, okay?"

"Your mom is coming from the airport with Will and Susan," Mike said. "We'll all be there to applaud for you and Melanie."

"Thanks, Dad," Christina said, then headed out the door.

This is the last time I'll be parking here, Christina thought as she stopped the Blazer in the high school lot. She carried her plastic-shrouded cap and gown across the grounds to the auditorium, where the seniors were gathering in the band room. Christina joined the throng, smiling distractedly at several of her classmates. Most of them looked as nervous as she felt. *At least I'm not the only one with end-of-school jitters*, she thought as she made her way through the crowd.

She saw Melanie and Katie in a corner of the room and headed in that direction. The other two girls were already wearing their graduation gowns, and when Christina reached them, Katie gave her a friendly smile.

"Can you believe we're done with this place? It seems like we've been here for all eternity."

Christina wrinkled her nose. "I think I missed the

75

last couple of years," she admitted. "It kind of went by in a blur."

Katie looked at her steadily, then smiled in understanding. "I know," she said. "You've had a lot going on the last few years. I still miss riding together, you know."

"Me too," Christina said with a sigh. "I'm sorry about not having much time for you—and all my other friends," she added. "I didn't think about everyone disappearing after high school, but now I wish I'd been able to do more. I'm going to miss this." She gestured around the room, which was full of people she'd spent her school years with, from kindergarten on.

Impulsively Katie threw her arms around Christina, giving her a close hug. "I won't be too far away," she said. "You can track me down at the University of Kentucky campus, okay?"

"I will," Christina promised.

"Now get your gown on," Melanie said. "We need to get lined up pretty soon. You don't want to miss that, too."

Christina slipped on her gown and held up her arms, letting the wide sleeves flap. "I could have just worn one of the sleeves," she said with a laugh. "These things are huge."

"And very attractive," Katie added, handing her her cap. "Now remember, the tassel goes left to right."

"Or was that right to left?" Melanie threw in.

Christina rolled her eyes. "Don't confuse me," she exclaimed. "I'm doing good to remember how to walk. That's left foot, right foot, right?"

"We'll be fine," Katie said confidently.

Christina felt a twinge of envy. Katie was registering at the university, majoring in English, and didn't have to worry about figuring out what she was going to do until she graduated from college. Christina sighed to herself. Why had she ever thought getting away from school would be a good thing? Graduating from high school was like having the gate spring open at the start of a race, only instead of a nice oval track, she had to choose which direction she moved in, and she still didn't know which way to go.

Soon the group was lined up, ready to walk into the main hall. Christina marched out with her classmates, surprised at how crowded the auditorium was. She searched the room for her parents, finally locating them. Will and Susan were there with them, along with Tor and Samantha Nelson, and Cindy. To Christina's delight, Parker was also sitting with her parents.

Christina had been prepared to be bored during the speeches and award presentations, but to her surprise, the ceremony seemed to go by too fast. After the last senior had been handed his diploma, the hall erupted into applause. Christina hugged her certificate to her chest. First she needed to get through the Belmont with Star; then she would get on with the next part of her life, which more and more seemed as though it would involve college. But which one, and what to study, still eluded her. Veterinary work sounded interesting, but was she up to working as hard as Dani did, taking so much math and science? She really didn't know.

After going through the receiving line, she headed for the parking lot. Most of the seniors were attending a class party, but Christina hadn't signed up for the festivities, knowing she had Star to take care of and the Belmont ahead of her. Her parents had made reservations at an Italian restaurant in Lexington, so after an early evening, she would head home for a good night's sleep.

Melanie was also skipping the class party. Now that she was riding Gratis, she, too, had a very early morning the next day. She and her parents were having dinner with the Reeses. When Christina reached the parking lot, Parker was waiting near the driver's door of the Blazer.

"Thanks for coming," she said, giving him a quick hug. "I was so glad to see you in the audience."

"I didn't want to miss your graduation," he said with a grin, pulling a bouquet of flowers from behind his back. He gazed down at her. "I've missed a lot of things," he said.

"Me too," Christina replied, accepting the flowers. "Thank you, Parker. They're beautiful." She suddenly felt shy, and she ducked her head to sniff the bouquet. "This was thoughtful."

"Your parents invited me to go to dinner with all of you," Parker said. "I hope you don't mind."

"Mind?" Christina shook her head. "That would be so great."

"I'll meet you at the restaurant," Parker said. "My truck is parked in the visitors' lot."

By the time Christina reached the restaurant, her parents were already there. She walked in and saw them seated at a large table. Melanie was sitting next to her father and stepmother. She waved when she saw Christina, who hurried to the table. She sat down across from Samantha and Tor.

"Is Cindy coming?" she asked.

Ashleigh shook her head. "She had to get back to Tall Oaks," she said. "They're getting Gratis ready to take up to New York tomorrow, and she had things to take care of."

"When are we taking Star?" Christina asked.

"We'll head up there on Monday," her mother replied as Parker walked up to the table. He pulled out the empty chair next to Christina and sat down.

"Hi, everyone," he said. "It's been ages since I saw you," he commented to Samantha and Tor.

"Right," Tor drawled. "Since this afternoon when you were at Whisperwood with your horses."

"How are you feeling?" Parker asked Samantha.

She smiled brightly. "Perfect," she said.

Christina looked closely at Samantha and frowned. Samantha seemed a little too pale to be feeling perfect, she thought. "Is something wrong?" she asked.

Samantha caught her lower lip in her teeth, then glanced at Tor. "I wanted to wait to make the announcement," she said. "This is your and Melanie's graduation party."

"If there's some big news you have to share, tell us now," Melanie demanded, leaning forward and giving Samantha a determined look. "No fair keeping secrets."

Tor glanced at Samantha and gave her a smile. "I

guess now is as good a time as any to share the news," he said.

"You tell them," Samantha said, smiling back at her husband.

Tor nodded, then picked up a spoon and tapped the side of his water glass, even though there was no conversation going at the table. "Samantha and I have a big announcement," he said. "We're expecting an addition to the family."

Christina looked at them blankly. "You got Sterling bred?" she asked.

Both Tor and Samantha burst into laughter, and Melanie leaped from her chair. "You're going to have a baby!" she exclaimed, darting around the table to throw her arms around Samantha.

"Yes, we are, and we wanted to share the news with you all at once," Samantha said. "I just wish Cindy and Ben could have been here, but we'll tell them tomorrow."

Christina gaped at Samantha. "A baby," she repeated, stunned by the news. "That's wonderful!"

After the waitress had taken their orders, the conversation centered on Tor and Samantha's baby.

"She's going to be a jockey," Melanie said, taking a breadstick from a basket the waitress had set on the table.

"He's going to be a steeplechaser," Tor replied, leaning back in his chair.

"Maybe you'll have twins, and they can do three-day eventing," Parker threw in.

Samantha laughed. "I guess we'll just have to wait and see," she said.

"Speaking of eventing, how are things going with Ozzie and Foxy?" Ashleigh asked Parker.

Parker's face lit up. "Great. Jack Dalton is really pushing us," he said. "And the horses seem to love it. I know we'll make it onto the U.S. team for the next Olympics."

Christina glanced at him and raised her eyebrows. "Is Jack Dalton pushing their rider, too?"

At that Parker rolled his eyes. "I can stay in the saddle," he said. "But I think Foxy and Ozzie could run a course even without a rider."

Samantha was nodding in agreement. "The time and effort you've put into their training really shows, Parker," she said. "I know Captain Donnelly is happy with the progress you've made."

Tor picked up a breadstick and pointed it at Parker. "Just remember you have classes starting in the fall, too," he said.

Parker sighed. "I'll be back from England before classes start," he said.

"We're very proud of you, but we do miss you at Whisperwood," Samantha said.

"I know," Parker said. "You're going to need me there to teach that baby to ride."

Everyone laughed at the comment. Christina was relieved that the focus of the talk was not on her future, and she was sure Melanie felt the same way. Soon the food arrived, and after a pleasant meal and relaxed conversation, they ended graduation evening early.

Parker walked Christina to the Blazer. "I've really missed you a lot, Chris," he said. "Maybe after the summer we can spend more time together."

Christina shrugged. "I'd like that," she admitted. "But I still don't know what I'm going to be doing."

"Why don't you go over to the university campus?" Parker suggested. "You could check out the facilities and think a little more about taking some classes. Not that I'm trying to push you," he added quickly. "I know how I felt when my dad was practically shoving college down my throat. I had to make that decision on my own, but it would be pretty cool if you were around the campus. We'd be able to see each other every day." He smiled at her. "Maybe that's a bit of an incentive for you."

Christina sighed. "Let me get through the Belmont," she said. "Then I'll do some serious thinking about it."

"Fair enough," Parker said. He leaned down and gave her a soft kiss on the lips, then a quick hug. "I need to get home," he said. "I have an early meeting tomorrow with Captain Donnelly."

"Thanks for coming to graduation," Christina said. "I'll see you later."

When she got home Christina went straight to the barn, walking down the wide aisle to Star's stall. When she reached his stall, she saw that Dani had groomed him to perfection. There was a box on the floor outside the stall addressed to Christina and Star. Curious, she picked it up. Star stuck his nose over the door and nudged the package.

"I know it's for both of us, but I'll open it," she told him. The card inside the box was from Dani, congratulating her on graduation and wishing her luck at the Belmont. Beneath the card was a plastic bag of apple slices, and under that was a tissue-wrapped charm bracelet. Christina examined the trinkets hung from the bracelet. The first was a tiny silver horse, the second a graduation cap, the third a minute textbook, and the fourth a trophy. Christina fastened the bracelet to her wrist, then fed Star the apple pieces.

"Look," she told the colt, pointing at the horse charm dangling from the bracelet. "Here's you. Here I am, the graduate, and I guess the book and the trophy are supposed to be our future. We're going to win the Belmont." She sighed. "You are going to be a rocket on the track, aren't you?"

Star snorted, as if in agreement.

Christina tapped at the silver textbook charm and frowned to herself. "I take it Dani thinks I should be going to college. Parker wants me to go, Cindy thinks I should go, but Vince thinks I should race and put away money for the future." She grimaced, then looked at Star. "I still don't know what to do. It seems like I'm trying to make my decisions based on what everyone else is telling me. What I need to do is think this through for me. After all, it is my life, isn't it?"

In response, Star bobbed his head, then lipped her hands in search of another piece of apple. Christina handed him one and rubbed his nose while he chewed. "As long as you're well cared for and get to race, you're fine with whatever I do, right?"

Star grunted softly, and Christina chuckled. "Of course you are," she said. "Life is simple for you. You eat and you run and you don't worry about anything else. Worrying about our future is my job."

She strolled back up to the house, where her parents were already in bed. Will and Susan were spending the night at Townsend Acres with Melanie, who would be heading for New York with her parents, meeting Cindy at Belmont so that she could work with Gratis on the track.

Christina yawned as she shut off the kitchen light and headed upstairs. It had been a busy day. She didn't regret missing the senior class party, though she did wonder what other parts of her life were going to pass her by if she put all her energy and attention into racing and the track. But she loved the horses, and she couldn't imagine a life without them being a part of it. For the last few years, however, she'd been so busy with Star that she had no time for anything else. There had to be more to life than just the farm. Only she didn't know how to incorporate everything. There had to be a way, but she couldn't conceive of it.

6

When the Reeses pulled into the back parking lot at Belmont late Monday afternoon, Christina immediately went to the trailer to check on Star. The colt whinnied at her when she opened the trailer door, twisting his neck so that he could look at her as she stepped inside.

"How are you doing, boy?" she asked, quickly checking his shipping boots. Star shifted his weight and tugged at the trailer tie, clearly impatient to get out of the trailer. His movement rocked the trailer, and Christina patted his shoulder, pulling his blanket straight.

"I'll have you out in a minute," she said. "I just want to make sure you look your best when you get outside. When all the other horses see you make your entrance, we want them to know they're in the presence of royalty, right?" She hooked a lead line to his halter, unclipping the tie as she spoke.

Ashleigh was waiting when Christina led Star out of the trailer. The colt arched his neck and raised his nose to test the air. He pricked his ears, flared his nostrils, and whinnied loudly, dancing excitedly in place as he took in the scents of the Belmont backside.

Ashleigh smiled at Christina. "He knows where he is," she said.

"He's telling the competition that Wonder's Star is here and they'd all better watch out," Christina replied, patting Star's tense neck.

"We'll put him on the track tomorrow morning," Ashleigh said. "He's had a few days of rest, so I'm sure he'll be pretty energetic."

Christina led the colt through the security gate and toward the rows of stalls that lined the track's backside. As they walked along the shed rows, she checked out some of the horses being kept at the track. Most of the Thoroughbreds were there for less renowned races than the Belmont, but Christina was still impressed with the array of well-bred racehorses she saw.

In spite of the late hour, the backside was still busy

with grooms, trainers, owners, and jockeys visiting and working. As she led Star through the aisles, people stopped talking and gazed at the colt. Christina raised her chin, smiling to herself at the awed sounds she heard and the long looks that Star was getting. *These are people who know horses,* she told herself. *And they can see the quality in Star.* She leaned a little closer to her excited colt.

"They know you're a celebrity," she murmured. She shook her head, reminding herself of the significance of Star's nomination into the Triple Crown races. Although she always believed that Star was the greatest horse in the world, she thought that was simply because of the special relationship she had with him.

Christina saw the banner for Celtic Meadows and she slowed Star, peering at Wild 'n' Free's stall. She could see the colt's outline, and smiled and nodded at the colt's caretaker as she led Star on. In front of them, a slender woman came out of another stall and started down the aisle.

"Ugh," Christina muttered to herself when she recognized Alexis Huffman and saw Speed.com in the stall. Alexis had worked for Tall Oaks when Fredericka Graber owned the farm. She had made herself a lot of money, and driven Fredericka nearly to bankruptcy, when she was the farm manager. Alexis had disappeared for several months, only to resurface as the trainer for Speed.com, the horse owned by Dustin Gates, a wealthy businessman. Christina ignored Speed.com's trainer and checked the stall numbers, looking for Whitebrook's area.

"Right here, Chris." Dani waved to her, and Christina led Star to the groom. Dani had driven up the day before to prepare the stall for Star's arrival.

"I don't suppose you could have asked for a better neighborhood," Christina said to Dani, nodding toward the stall Alexis had just exited.

Dani curled her lip. "Nothing against Dustin Gates and his horse," she said. "But being this close to Alexis for the next week doesn't sound like fun. And check that out." She pointed across the aisle. "Look who else is moving in."

Directly across from Star's stall, a groom was hanging a green-and-gold sign for Townsend Acres. "Oh, well," Christina said. "It could be worse."

"How?" Dani inquired.

Christina grinned at the groom and raised her shoulders. "I don't know," she said. "But there has to be some way it could be worse."

"Let me know when you figure it out," Dani said.

"We'll have to listen to Brad holding court for all of Celtic Mist's admirers for the next few days." Then a slow grin spread across her face. "On second thought," she said, "I won't." She dug into the duffel bag sitting beside her chair and held up a personal stereo. She dangled the headphones. "I can listen to music and books on tape. Brad's lips may be moving, but I'll be grooving to a different sound."

"Smart move," Christina said with a laugh.

"Welcome to Belmont." At the sound of Cindy's voice, Christina turned to see the Tall Oaks trainer walking up the middle of the aisle. "I see you've met your neighbors," Cindy said with a wry grin.

Christina nodded. "Where is your stall?" she asked.

Cindy tilted her head toward the next row of stalls. "Two rows over," she said. "We've got Magnifique in the stall beside Gratis. Del's trainer had a family emergency and won't be here until later in the week. Poor Del is pretty wound up over having his colt running in the Belmont. Ben and I thought we'd take him under our wing, so to speak."

Christina nodded in understanding. "After I get Star taken care of I want to go see Magnifique up close," she said.

"I'll be waiting for you," Cindy replied. She walked away as Christina and Dani set to work getting Star into his stall. When Christina stepped outside, Alexis was standing in front of Speed.com's stall, staring at her. Determined not to let the woman bother her, Christina gave a small wave in greeting. Alexis glared at her for a moment, then turned away and strode toward the track. Christina shook her head, still baffled by the idea that Dustin Gates had hired someone like Alexis to train his racehorse. But Alexis did know horses, and she was a capable trainer. She just didn't have any scruples that Christina was aware of.

Dani settled back onto her folding chair as Ashleigh walked up the aisle. "Does Star approve of his stall?" she asked, reaching over the door to give the colt a quick pat.

"He's fine," Christina said. She tilted her head toward Speed.com's stall. "Did you see Alexis?"

Ashleigh nodded. "I don't trust her one bit," she said flatly. "We'll keep a close eye on Star all week." She smiled at Christina. "I'll take first watch, if you want to check out some of the other horses."

"I'm going over to the Tall Oaks stalls," Christina said, pausing to give Star's velvety nose a kiss. "I need to have a little talk with Magnifique about running slow on Saturday."

"I'd like to wander around and check things out," Dani said. "I'm having a terrible craving for a burger from the track kitchen. Do you mind Star-sitting?"

"I'll be right here," Ashleigh promised.

Dani headed for the cafeteria, while Christina walked down the shed rows to Ben and Cindy's stable area, where Del Abdullah was standing with Cindy and another woman. Beckie was leaning against Gratis's stall door.

"I'd like you to meet Karen Taylor," Cindy said when Christina reached them.

"Seattle Slew's owner," Christina said, reaching out to shake the woman's hand. "What an honor to meet you."

Karen smiled warmly. "You know, last winter when your colt was so ill, then recovered to come back and run in the Triple Crown, it reminded me of Slew."

"You mean when he got sick at Hialeah?" Cindy asked.

Karen nodded. "Doug Peterson had him down there late in the year," she said. "The horse next to him got sick, and even though Doug moved him, Slew still nearly died."

"But he came back to race again," Christina said. "Just like Star."

"Oh, yes," Karen said. "For him to come back and

run so well after that illness was pretty remarkable, but your Star has done even better. Slew's trainer always said our colt was a survivor with the heart of a true champion. I think you could say the same thing about Wonder's Star." She gestured at Magnifique. "I could hardly wait to meet Magnifique," she said. "I love seeing Slew's descendants do well."

"He *is* an awesome horse," Christina agreed. "I've seen him move. He's going to be a bullet on the track Saturday."

Karen nodded. "But Star has something special, and I think the two of you will put on quite a show next weekend."

"Thank you," Christina said, warmed by the high praise from the owner of one of racing's greatest horses.

Karen glanced at her watch. "Jean Cruguet and I have an interview over at the grandstand in just a few minutes," she told Cindy. "The papers still can't seem to get enough stories about Seattle Slew."

"I'd love to meet him," Christina said quickly.

Del gave Christina a quizzical look. "Why does the name Jean Cruguet sound familiar?" he asked.

"He was Seattle Slew's jockey in the Triple Crown," Christina replied.

"I used to study tapes of his riding every chance I got when I was racing," Cindy added. "Jean always said he just got on and let the horse run, but the truth is, he knows how to get a horse to run its best for him."

"He certainly does," Karen agreed. "I'd better get over to the grandstand, but I had to come by to see your colt." She turned to Christina. "It was wonderful to meet you," she said. "Good luck on Saturday, to all of you."

After she left, Cindy turned to Del. "We need to plan to work Magnifique in the morning," she told him. "I've arranged an exercise rider for Magnifique until your trainer gets here to deal with things."

Del shot Cindy a worried look. "Is working him tomorrow a good idea?" he asked. "Maybe he needs to rest up and take it easy."

"He needs to work," Cindy said, offering the nervous owner a reassuring smile. "I'll have him do the same work Gratis will be doing. Your trainer called me early this morning, and we have everything under control."

"Thank you," Del said with a relieved sigh. "I think I'll go look at some of the other horses around here. I'm getting quite an education." He strolled down the row of stalls, looking carefully at each of the horses he passed, pausing to visit with the attendants as he went.

"Del's a little overwhelmed by everything that's going on," Christina said.

"He certainly is," Cindy agreed, shaking her head. "I've been around the horses and the track for so long, I started to take it all for granted."

"Seeing how it affects Del does put things in a different light, doesn't it?" Christina said.

"Is your mom here?" Cindy asked.

"She's at Star's stall right now," Christina replied. "I should go back and see if she needs anything."

"I'll walk with you," Cindy said.

"I'll stay right here with the horses," Beckie said. Gratis leaned his head out the door and swung it in her direction, and Beckie poked him in the jaw. "I'm not a snack for you," she said flatly. "Keep trying to bite me and I'll start feeding you Vegemite, you beast."

Cindy laughed. "If you did that and he won the Belmont, you'd have every trainer in the country feeding that nasty spread to their horses."

Beckie nodded. "I could start my own import business," she said. "Selling Vegemite in horse-size buckets."

"I'll be back soon," Cindy said, and she and

Christina walked away. When they reached White-brook's area, Christina saw a crowd gathered in front of Celtic Mist's stall.

"The Preakness winner must have arrived," Cindy said. "Brad knows how to orchestrate a media frenzy better than anyone I know."

As they got closer, Christina could see the top of Brad's head. Celtic Mist's owner was in the center of the knot of people, most of them obviously journalists, with their tape recorders and notebooks out, clinging to Brad's every word. She shook her head. "This is going to be a fun place to be for the next few days," she said to Cindy.

Ashleigh was standing in front of Star's stall. She eyed the throng at Celtic Mist's stall and gave Christina and Cindy a resigned smile. "At least with all the attention on Celtic Mist, Star won't be harassed by the media," she said. "I'm fine here if you two have other things to do for a while."

Christina looked from her mother to Cindy. "I wondered if the farm where Legacy is kept is nearby." Christina had heard that the stallion, once co-owned by Whitebrook and Townsend Acres, was standing at stud in New York.

Ashleigh's jaw dropped and her eyes went wide.

Christina folded her arms in front of her. "I'd just like to see how he's doing," she said.

"I didn't know you'd even thought much about Legacy since we sold the farm's interest in him," Ashleigh said. Ashleigh had given Christina Whitebrook's share of the colt with the hope that ownership of one of Wonder's foals would inspire Christina to start racing. But at the time Christina's heart had been set on eventing. She knew her mother had been deeply disappointed when she sold Legacy to buy Sterling Dream, and now that she was involved in racing, she had to wonder at her choice, too.

"I do think about him once in a while, Mom," Christina replied. She had thought Ashleigh would realize that even though the colt had not been the right horse for Christina, she still cared about him.

Cindy nodded in understanding. "I could take you to the breeding farm where he's standing," she offered, then looked at Ashleigh. "Unless you wanted to go. I could stay here and keep an eye on Star."

"No," Ashleigh said quickly. "You and Christina go ahead." She sat down in front of Star's stall. "Star and I will be fine right here."

Christina and Cindy walked to the back lot and climbed into Cindy's car.

"I wonder why your mom didn't want to go," Cindy commented.

"Maybe she's afraid Legacy will remind her too much of Wonder," Christina said. "If I'd kept Legacy, she might not have bred Wonder again." She sighed. "Wonder might still be alive, but I wouldn't have Star, either." After letting Legacy go, Ashleigh had made the choice to breed Wonder one last time, but giving birth to Star had cost the mare her life. Ashleigh had been devastated at the loss of her beloved Wonder. Christina hadn't truly understood the depth of the bond her mother had had with Wonder until she had experienced the same thing with Star.

Cindy started the car, and as they left the lot she shot a quizzical glance at Christina. "What made you decide to see Legacy?" she asked.

Christina stared out the windshield and shrugged. "I've been thinking a lot lately about the choices I've made the last few years," she said. "I know Mom was pretty disappointed when I gave up Legacy to buy Sterling Dream. But when I let go of my interest in him, racing was the last thing on my mind. Now I'd just like to know that he's doing okay."

Cindy headed down the road. "The place isn't too far," she said. They drove several miles to reach the breeding farm where Wonder's Legacy was standing at stud. When Cindy pulled into the driveway and parked at the farm office, she looked around at the barns and nodded. "This looks like a decent facility," she commented.

To Christina, the barns didn't look particularly well maintained, and most of the pastures were fenced with wire instead of boards. But the pastures were clean and green, and there seemed to be plenty of room in the turnouts for the horses. Christina frowned. "I don't like this place," she said quietly.

"It isn't Whitebrook," Cindy agreed. "But not everybody feels as deeply about the horses as we do, remember."

"I know," Christina said, struggling with a sense of guilt over her part in having one of Ashleigh's Wonder's offspring live in such a place. "I'm glad Mom didn't come with us," she said. "I don't think she'd be too impressed."

Cindy sighed. "Let's see if we can take a look at Legacy," she said, climbing from the car.

Christina followed her to the barn office. The woman in the office greeted them warmly and seemed sincerely happy to meet Christina.

"We love Legacy," she said. "He's got such a pleasant personality. I'd be happy to show him to you."

Christina and Cindy followed her to a large barn. In spite of the exterior neglect, the barn was clean and well lit. Christina walked down the aisle, looking carefully at the horses they passed. Each of the animals appeared well cared for, but she could see that the caliber of horses at the breeding farm was nowhere near the quality of racehorses she was used to.

When they reached Legacy's stall, the chestnut horse raised his head and gave them an indifferent look, then turned his attention back to a flake of hay someone had put down for him.

"See?" the woman said. "He's such an easygoing horse. We like having him here. He isn't at all high-strung or difficult to work with. Legacy is a real gentleman."

Christina stepped close to the stall. She could see the difference between Legacy and the other horses here at first glance. Besides having the powerful build of a well-bred Thoroughbred, Legacy had the perfectly formed head and graceful neck that both he and Star had gotten from their dam. The horse looked perfectly fine and healthy.

Christina reached out and let the stallion snuffle her fingers, and she ran her hand down his sleek nose. "You're doing okay, aren't you, boy?"

The stallion looked past her and blew out noisily,

then turned away to take another bite of hay. Christina heaved a sigh and looked at Cindy. "I guess we can go now," she said, then turned to the woman. "Thanks for letting us see him."

"Anytime you want to come back, feel welcome," she told them as they left the barn.

Christina was quiet on the drive back to Elmont. "I never should have let him go," she finally said.

"I think he looked good, Chris," Cindy replied. "He's well cared for and well fed. Maybe he doesn't get as much attention as the horses at Whitebrook and Tall Oaks, but most places don't treat their horses the way we do."

Christina nodded, sighing deeply. "If I hadn't been such a flake when I was younger, he'd still be at Whitebrook."

Cindy reached over and rested her hand on Christina's arm. "Don't you start feeling guilty about Legacy," she said quickly.

"But I gave him up without a thought," Christina protested.

"You were being forced to make a decision that you weren't ready to make," Cindy countered. "Your mom wanted so badly for you to become a jockey that she pushed it, instead of letting you get into racing in your own time." She smiled. "Legacy isn't being abused, he isn't in any danger, and they really seem to care about him, Chris," she continued. "We showed up without any warning, and the farm owners had nothing to hide from us. Legacy is all right."

Christina nodded. Cindy was right, but still, Legacy hadn't looked content. He didn't have that bright, satisfied expression that she read on Star's face when she saw him.

When they returned to the track, she rushed from the car, in a hurry to get back to Star's stall. But the guard at the back gate stopped her as she started to walk past him.

"I need to check your identification before I let you in," he said, scowling at Christina.

She dug into her pocket and pulled out her jockey's license and handed it to him. The guard examined it closely, then stared hard at her. "You own that chestnut colt that's been entered in the Belmont, right?"

"Yes," Christina said as Cindy reached the gate.

"I'll need to see your ID, too," the guard said to Cindy.

"What's going on?" Cindy asked, frowning at the serious expression on the guard's face. "Where's the regular gate guard? I've known him forever, since I was racing here years ago."

"We have a serious problem," the guard said, looking from Cindy to Christina, his face grim. "There's been an incident involving one of the horses being kept at your shed row."

"What happened?" Christina demanded, her heart starting to speed up as she thought of Star.

The guard frowned at both of them and shook his head. "We don't know how, but one of the Thoroughbreds has been stolen."

CHRISTINA AND CINDY SHOT EACH OTHER LOOKS OF
horror.

"Star," Christina gasped, a jolt of fear surging
through her.

"Gratis," Cindy said at the same time, her eyes
wide.

Before the guard could react, Christina and Cindy
dashed through the gate and ran between the shed
rows toward their horses' stalls. Christina's mind
reeled at the idea of Star being gone. The thought of
someone taking her colt, the possibility of somebody
mistreating him, gave wings to her feet. Her heart
thudded painfully in her chest, and she struggled to
keep her panicky emotions under control.

As they neared the area where their horses were kept, Christina saw Melanie hurrying in their direction. Her heart sank at the tense expression on her cousin's face. It was Star who had been taken. She knew it. Her mind darted ahead to an image of his empty stall, and she nearly burst into tears. "Star!" she cried out.

"It wasn't Star," Melanie called. She shook her head in a firm no. "Star and Gratis are both fine," she added as she got closer. "I just came from Gratis's stall. Beckie is sitting with him, making sure no one gets close enough to so much as touch a whisker on his nose. And Dani is with Star."

Christina and Cindy slowed as Melanie's message sank in. Star was all right. Christina's heart was still hammering and the adrenaline in her system made her feel shaky, but rather than terror for her colt's well-being, she felt dizzy with the relief that rushed through her. The panicky feeling subsided at the news that Star was safe.

"That's good to hear," Cindy said, her voice expressing her relief. "But which horse was taken?"

"Speed.com," Melanie said. "They're wondering if someone is going to hold him for ransom."

Cindy frowned, then gave a small shrug. "With Dustin Gates's money, it isn't an impossible idea. But kidnapping a racehorse right off the track? Someone would have to be pretty desperate to take that kind of risk."

"Most of the owners and trainers are in a meeting with track security right now," Melanie said. "Ashleigh went, and so did Vince. I stuck around so I could let you guys know what's going on."

"Good," Cindy said, but then she frowned again and shook her head. "I wonder how someone managed to walk off with a racehorse in broad daylight. There's so much security around here, you couldn't even walk out with a bale of hay without having it checked."

Melanie raised her hands in a gesture of surrender. "It's all a mystery," she said. "Speed.com disappeared shortly after the morning works. No one remembers seeing him after his groom took him to the wash rack after his workout. And the groom is missing, too. Alexis is in a private meeting with the track officials right now," she added. "She was hysterical when she found out Dustin Gates's colt was gone."

Gradually Christina's heart rate slowed as she absorbed the news. With Melanie and Cindy beside her, she walked to Star's stall. When they passed Speed.com's empty stall, a thought flickered in Christina's mind, then disappeared. She frowned, trying to catch the faint memory. There was something she knew about Speed.com that she needed to remember, but whatever it was eluded her.

Dani was sitting in a folding chair at the doorway of Star's stall, a paperback novel in her hands. Star had his head out the door, his nose on Dani's shoulder.

"He's reading now," she told Christina with a smile.

Christina gave the colt a loving pet, relief making her feel almost weak. "Thank goodness it wasn't Star," she murmured, stroking his neck. "I'd be frantic if something happened to you."

A loud, angry voice distracted them, and at the same time they all looked in the direction of the Townsend Acres stalls. Brad was striding along the aisle between the rows of stalls, a security official hurrying beside him. Brad was scowling deeply.

"This situation is completely unacceptable," Brad said loudly. He stopped near Celtic Mist's stall, his hands propped on his hips while he glowered at a track official.

"Heads are going to roll around here," Brad snarled, glaring down at the short man, who was wearing a Belmont track security staff jacket. "I'm not satisfied with that little meeting you held, trying to appease the owners with some pathetic reassurance. Your staff is incompetent." He angled his head and narrowed his eyes. "They're completely inept."

Christina felt sorry for the security manager. She knew that if it had been Star who had been taken, she would be upset, but still, Brad was way out of line. Celtic Mist stuck his head out of his stall, his gray ears pricked in the direction of Brad's strident voice.

"I want some answers," Brad snapped. "And I want them now. Immediately."

"Mr. Townsend," the security manager said, "if you will just slow down—"

"This is totally unacceptable," Brad said, cutting the other man off. "If you can't protect the most valuable horses in the country with the current security setup, I demand that the track provide a twenty-four-hour guard posted at my horse's stall." He took a step closer to the other man and pointed a finger at his chest. "You will deal with this immediately." The security man took a step back as Brad leaned even closer.

He shook his head. "Mr. Townsend . . . ," he began.

Christina was impressed with how controlled his voice was. She knew if Brad had come unglued at her like that, she wouldn't have taken it so calmly.

The security manager raised his hands in a placating gesture. "Before you try throwing your weight around—"

"Throwing my weight around!" Brad exclaimed. "I've had it. I'll have your job before this is over!"

"You know what?" the security manager asked, finally sounding tired of Brad's relentless tirade. "You can have my job." He peeled off his jacket and dropped it at Brad's feet. Before Brad could respond, the man turned and walked away.

Brad's face turned beet red. "You get back here!" he yelled, kicking at the jacket.

Christina cringed at the sight. She had never seen Brad in such a state, and it was a little unnerving. She glanced at Melanie, who was gazing at Brad, a stunned look on her face.

"I think Brad's going to blow a gasket," Christina murmured, gripping Cindy's arm.

"He's got the right to be very upset," Melanie said, but she sounded a little uncertain. "He's worried for Celtic Mist's safety," she added hesitantly.

Brad finally looked around and seemed to come to his senses. When he saw all the people in the area staring in his direction, he spun on his heel and stormed away, his fists still tightly clenched.

Cindy looked at Brad, then at Melanie. "Maybe before Brad starts mouthing off he should get more information," she told Melanie. "Nothing gives him the right to go off like that. Nothing. He's no better than any other owner here." Cindy gave Melanie a long, steady look. "I can certainly understand being worried and upset," she continued. "But throwing a tantrum like that was completely uncalled for. Is that going to help anything?"

Melanie sighed. "I guess you're right," she said, turning to run her hand along Star's neck.

Christina rubbed Star's nose thoughtfully. "It seems odd that of all the horses, Speed.com is the one who was taken."

"You mean because Alexis is his trainer?" Melanie asked, meeting Christina's eyes.

"With her in the picture, anything could be going on," Cindy said. "They'll get to the bottom of it soon enough." She looked toward Speed.com's empty stall. "I'm sure they'll have the police here questioning everyone. In fact, I'd better get over to Gratis's stall and make sure everything is in order there. I'll see you two later." She strode away, leaving Christina and Melanie with Dani in front of Star's stall.

Christina looked from Melanie to Star, then back at

her cousin. Melanie's face was a little pale.

"Brad's been so pleasant to me," Melanie said softly. "It's easy to forget that he's used to getting his way, and when he doesn't, it isn't nice to be around him."

Christina exhaled heavily. "I wouldn't want him in my face like that," she said. "Brad can definitely be pretty intimidating."

Melanie dropped her gaze, staring at the toes of her paddock boots. "I guess I'd better be a little careful about what kind of deal I get into with Brad," she said.

Christina reached over and gave Melanie's hand a squeeze. "I know that Mom and Dad would be glad to have you and Image back at Whitebrook," she said. "Maybe we don't have a therapy pool, but we don't have Brad, either."

Melanie nodded. "I'll talk to Jazz this afternoon," she said. "I'm not sure what to do at this point." Her attention shifted to the end of the shed row, and she wrinkled her nose. "There's Alexis now," she said.

Christina looked up to see the trainer walking toward them. Alexis's mouth was pinched into a tight line, and she was walking rapidly, a scowl creasing her forehead.

"She doesn't exactly look distraught," Christina

said. "She looks a little more ticked off than upset."

"Yeah, that isn't the look I'd expect on someone who just lost a million-dollar racehorse," Melanie agreed.

As Alexis passed them, she shot a hard look at Christina and Melanie, then hurried past. She slowed when she reached Speed.com's unoccupied stall and stepped inside, coming out just a minute later. She strode off, shoving her hands into her pockets, and headed for the back parking lot. Christina watched her walk away and shook her head. "I wonder what she's up to," she muttered.

"Whatever it is, you know it's no good," Melanie replied. "Remember, that's the same woman who almost ruined Fredericka."

Ashleigh walked up to them, shaking her head. "The meeting wasn't too productive," she said. "No one has any answers as to how someone walked out of here with Speed.com. Alexis seemed very upset after her meeting with the officials, and I understand that." She smiled thinly at Christina and Melanie. "I know she isn't exactly an honorable character," she said. "But I don't think she walked away with Dustin Gates's racehorse."

Melanie and Christina glanced at each other, but by

some unspoken agreement they said nothing to Ashleigh about their suspicions.

Ashleigh glanced at her watch. "I'm going to go call Ian and your dad," she told Christina. "I want to let them know what's going on here, and go over Star's works with Ian." She left Melanie and Christina standing in the aisle and hurried off.

Christina gazed across the aisle at Celtic Mist's stall, and suddenly she realized what had been bothering her about Speed.com. "Oh," she said, grabbing Melanie's shoulder. "I wonder . . ." Her voice faded as she struggled to recall the details of the last time she had watched Dustin Gates's colt work on the track.

"What?" Melanie asked, giving Christina a searching look.

"Before the Preakness," Christina said, glancing around to make certain no one but Melanie and Dani could hear her. "Speed.com didn't look like he was moving soundly. I thought then that he looked like he was starting to go lame."

Melanie's jaw dropped and she stared at Christina. "You don't think . . ."

Christina worked her jaw and looked in the direction of Speed.com's stall. "With Alexis running the show, it wouldn't surprise me if she had the colt stolen to cover up a soundness problem."

"That's hard to imagine," Melanie said, but she was nodding. "And just the kind of thing Alexis would do."

"If she was medicating him to keep it a secret, she'd be in trouble if he did well enough in the Belmont to be drug-tested," Dani commented.

"But whom could we talk to about it?" Christina asked. "I can't go around making accusations like that."

Melanie frowned thoughtfully. "Together we can figure something out," she said. "Right now I need to go talk to Cindy about Gratis's works for the next couple of days. Then we'll get together and talk about this." Her eyes lit up, and she gave Christina a conspiratorial wink. "If there's something underhanded going on with Alexis Huffman," she said, "we'll catch her."

After Melanie left, Christina wandered along the shed row, looking at the Thoroughbreds, her mind on Alexis and the missing horse. If she were Alexis, where would she take Speed.com? She couldn't imagine what someone would do with a stolen racehorse, and didn't know where to begin trying to solve the mystery.

But one good thing that was coming of this was that she and Melanie were doing something together. If nothing ever came of trying to find out if Alexis was the culprit in Speed.com's disappearance, maybe it would help heal her friendship with Melanie.

8

"I LOVE THIS TIME OF THE DAY," CHRISTINA SAID ON Wednesday morning as she buckled her helmet into place. Dani held Star, whose attention was fixed on the track, while Beckie kept a firm grip on Gratis's lead and Melanie checked his girth. The sun was just a suggestion of a glow on the horizon, while the vapor lights along the inside of the oval illuminated the racetrack with their pale radiance. Although the June air had a slight nip to it, Christina was comfortable in a light sweatshirt. Once she and Star started working, they'd both warm up quickly.

There was already another horse working in the predawn hour, but Christina knew that soon the track would be much busier. She liked being one of the first riders in the morning, getting Star's works in before there was too much traffic in and around the track and the backside.

Melanie looked up and nodded. "This is the best part of the day," she said. "I wasn't much of a morning person until I moved to Whitebrook. Now I can't imagine missing sunup."

Beckie gave her a leg up onto Gratis's back and unclipped his lead line. "I'm lucky to have a job where I get to enjoy the sunrise every morning," she said, giving the colt a pat on the shoulder.

Christina smiled. It was good to see Beckie back to her old, perky self. Obviously she was over the little crush she'd had on Wolf.

Dani gave Christina a boost onto Star's saddle. The colt snorted and took a sideways step toward the track.

"Hang on, fellow," Dani said, keeping Star under control while Christina adjusted her stirrups and collected her reins.

"Thanks," she said to Dani. "I think we're good to go now." Dani released Star's head, and Christina pointed him toward the gap in the rail. "Let's hit the track." Star snorted and tugged at the bit, eager to get to work.

"He does love to run, doesn't he?" Dani commented.

Christina nodded. "You live for this, don't you, boy?" she asked Star. Star pranced excitedly, crab-walking in his eagerness to move out as she rode him onto the track, Gratis close behind him.

Christina and Melanie began walking the horses to warm them up, riding counterclockwise so that the horses wouldn't immediately set their minds to racing. After a few strides, Christina glanced at her cousin, who was sitting deep in the saddle, her full attention on the bay colt. Gratis suddenly stiffened his legs and crow-hopped a few times. Melanie quickly got the feisty racehorse under control and urged him forward.

Christina laughed. "He's just full of himself, isn't he?"

"Oh, yeah," Melanie said, tightening the reins as Gratis flung his head forward and struck out with his front legs, trying to tear himself free. "He's going to be right at the front of the pack on Saturday. I'm so glad Cindy asked me to ride for Ben and her." She took a deep breath, then released a heavy sigh. "I only wish it were Image and not him I was racing." She darted a look at Christina. "And I do wish you and Star the best, you know."

"I know," Christina said, sighing as she thought of the competition Star was up against in the Belmont. The race was going to be a challenge. "Have you talked to the vets about how Image is doing?"

Melanie shook her head. "I talked to Jazz last night about moving her, but he doesn't want to push her recovery any more than I do. I know she's going to be fine, though," she added. "The vets Brad has coming to work with her are really good doctors. And in spite of Brad's obnoxious behavior, we're still lucky that he's letting us use Townsend Acres."

"I know the doctors are concerned about what's best for Image, but they're still working for Brad," Christina pointed out, squeezing her legs against Star's sides to move him into a jog.

"That's the biggest problem," Melanie said, pushing Gratis's pace up a notch so that she and Christina were riding side by side. "I talked to Jazz about having our own vet look at her, and he agrees. I just don't want to offend Brad. I'd hate to move Image before she's really ready to go." She stared between Gratis's alert ears. "No matter what it costs."

"Are you sure?" Christina asked.

Melanie shrugged, focusing on Gratis as he tried to rear up. She leaned forward, urging the colt to keep moving ahead. He settled down again and Melanie glanced at Christina. "Even if it means giving up Image's first foal," she said, conviction strong in her voice.

Christina nodded in understanding. Melanie knew she was welcome to bring Image back to Whitebrook, so Christina let the subject drop, not wanting to push the issue with her cousin. Whitebrook didn't have anything like Townsend Acres' rehabilitation facility, and Christina knew that if it was Star who needed the intense therapy that Image required, she'd be torn, too.

"Have you thought any more about Alexis and Speed.com?" she asked.

"I haven't stopped," Melanie said, then laughed. "Well, maybe for a few minutes while I was on the phone with Jazz," she admitted.

"He'll be here for the race, won't he?" Christina asked.

"He promised," Melanie said. "He has to be in Los Angeles Thursday and then needs to be in Seattle on Sunday, so he has a couple of days to spend with me." She glanced at Christina. "What about Parker? Is he going to be up here for the race?"

Christina looked straight ahead, gazing at the wide track in front of her. "I don't know," she said. "I'm not sure when he's going back to England. Besides, with the field that's going to be running on Saturday, Star probably won't have much of a shot at winning anyway. Parker doesn't need to stick around here to watch us lose, when he could be training."

"That's a defeatist attitude!" Melanie exclaimed. "Magnifique and Wild 'n' Free have some of the same bloodlines that Gratis has. I know Gratis will rock, and Star can beat him, which means Star stands a good chance of beating the other two. I don't think the rest of the field is anywhere near the caliber of our horses."

"Thanks, Mel," Christina said, pleased by the encouragement.

"As far as Speed.com goes," Melanie added, "if you're right and he was starting to go lame, it would make sense that Alexis would do something sneaky, like have him disappear. If she made a mistake in his training and caused him some type of injury, she'd need to cover it up."

"But where would she take him?" Christina asked, posting to Star's smooth trot. "If you were going to steal a Thoroughbred, what would you do with him?"

"I'd hide him in plain sight," Melanie said without hesitating.

"You mean like that story in the papers a few years back about the missing broodmare?" Christina asked.

"The one they found in someone's backyard pasture?"

"Exactly," Melanie replied. "The dam of a famous racehorse vanishes, and all the while she's in plain sight." They neared the gap at the end of the oval, where Ashleigh and Cindy were waiting, clipboards in hand.

"Just keep jogging Star," Ashleigh told Christina when she slowed Star near the rail. "Gallop him a little, then cool him down, and we'll keep him off the track until Saturday."

Christina nodded and rode Star off as Cindy gave Melanie her instructions for the rest of Gratis's work. As Christina trotted Star along the outside rail, another rider brought a horse onto the track. Christina recognized Celtic Meadows' chestnut colt, Wild 'n' Free. The exercise rider gave her a nod as he jogged his mount, keeping pace with Star.

"I'm Justin Powers," he said, offering her a friendly grin.

"Christina Reese," she replied, returning his smile.

"I know," Justin said. "I've watched you race. You're really good."

"Thanks," Christina said. "You did a great job with Wild 'n' Free in the Preakness. That was some impressive riding."

The grin stretching across Justin's face grew even

broader. "I've been riding on the West Coast for years," he said. "I was lucky to get a chance to race for Ghyllian Hollis's stable. What a privilege to ride in the Triple Crown. I still can't believe I get to do it."

Christina immediately liked the other jockey. Justin was stockily built and broad-shouldered for a jockey, but he sat his horse lightly, using quiet hands to control Wild 'n' Free as they moved around the track.

The riders fell silent, and Christina began mulling over the story about the stolen Thoroughbred mare. What if Speed.com was being kept somewhere near Belmont? What if Alexis did have something to do with the colt's disappearance? There wasn't much she and Melanie could do. Dustin Gates had probably hired professional detectives to search for Speed.com. She and Melanie knew horses, but they certainly didn't know how to do police work. She rested her hands on Star's sweaty neck and slowed the colt.

"See you later," she said to Justin, heading Star off the track.

Dani was waiting with a cooling sheet, which she threw over Star's back when Christina pulled the saddle off. "Do you want me to walk him out?" the groom asked.

"That'd be great," Christina said. "I want to go

shower and have some breakfast before the track kitchen gets too crowded."

Dani led Star away and Christina headed for the lockers.

By the time she was done showering, Melanie was walking into the locker room. "Do you feel like playing detective?" she asked.

Christina started to say no but caught herself. This was a chance for her and Melanie to do something together, even if it was as pointless as trying to solve the mystery of Speed.com's theft. "Sure," she said agreeably, not at all sure that they should be doing anything.

"When I lived here," Melanie said, "there was an old farm not far away that was pretty run-down. I heard it's abandoned now. If I were going to sneak a horse off the track, I'd take him there until I could move him farther away without attracting a lot of attention."

"How do we get there?" Christina asked. "It wouldn't exactly be discreet to drive around in a taxi, would it?"

Melanie rolled her eyes. "I already asked Cindy if we could borrow her car," she said.

"Did you tell her why?" Christina asked, surprised

that Cindy would agree to loan them her car to play private detective.

"I told her we're just going for a drive. I've never had a chance to show you around my old stomping grounds, okay?"

Christina shrugged. "Let me go check on Star, and I'll be ready to leave."

"I'll see you at the back parking lot in half an hour," Melanie said, heading for the showers.

Christina walked back to Star's stall to find him contently munching a flake of hay, his coat gleaming from the bath Dani had given him. Dani was sitting in front of the stall, her attention on the textbook she was holding. She glanced up to smile at Christina.

"He's a perfect gentleman," she said. "I just know you guys are going to be the greatest pair on the track on Saturday."

"Is that a completely unbiased point of view?" Christina asked with a laugh.

Dani pursed her lips, then grinned and shook her head. "Of course not," she replied. "But I know Star is one of the greatest horses I've ever seen run. He'll be the king of the track, I'm positive."

Christina gazed at her colt for a moment. Star flicked his ears at her and tore another mouthful of hay from his net, keeping his bright eyes fixed on her all the while. Christina flashed Dani a smile. "He thinks he's pretty hot stuff, too, don't you, boy?" She patted the colt's neck, then told Dani that she and Melanie were going for a drive.

Dani gave her a hard look. "If you happen to see a bay Thoroughbred standing around in someone's yard, make a note of the address and call the cops," she said.

"You aren't going to tell Mom or Cindy what we're doing, are you?" Christina asked.

Dani shook her head. "Just be careful, okay? If Alexis is desperate enough to steal a horse, who knows what else she might be capable of."

Christina nodded. "We're just going to keep an eye out," she said. "Melanie and I aren't going to take any big chances. We have horses to race on Saturday, remember?"

"Don't you forget," Dani said. "It's one thing to go look around, but with a valuable horse at stake, anything could happen."

"We'll be careful," Christina promised.

"Then good luck horse hunting," Dani said. "I'll be right here." She glanced over her shoulder at Star. "And I won't let Star out of my sight. I guarantee it."

"Thanks," Christina said. "I doubt there are going to be any more horse thefts here, but it's good to know Star will have the best guard at the track."

She walked away, feeling a little spark of excitement about venturing out with Melanie, even if it was nothing more than a wild-goose chase.

With Melanie at the wheel, the girls spent several hours driving the back roads in Elmont, the town surrounding the track. The abandoned farm Melanie had remembered had been leveled.

"So much for my great idea," Melanie said as they drove by the bare lot.

Christina stared out the window, trying to make herself think the way Alexis might—if, in fact, Speed.com had been taken by his trainer. She glanced at Melanie. "We're probably way off track," she said. "We don't like Alexis, but maybe she did clean up her act. It could very well be that Speed.com's groom was in cahoots with someone else, and they stole the colt. He could be anywhere in the United States by now."

Melanie grimaced, turning down a side road that ran past a large housing development. "I know it doesn't make any sense," she said, "but I still feel like Alexis is involved, and she hasn't had the time to get the colt moved anywhere far. I'm sure she's been watched."

"It's time to get back to Belmont," Christina said. "We need to stop and fill the gas tank for Cindy, and it's getting late."

After filling the gas tank, the girls started back toward the track. Melanie was quiet, and Christina was sure she was a little disappointed over not easily solving the mystery of Speed.com's disappearance.

She turned her head to gaze out the window, taking in a pasture filled with riding horses. Suddenly a jolt of surprise made her sit up straight. "Stop the car!" she cried.

Melanie jammed on the brakes and swerved onto the shoulder. "What?" she demanded. "What's wrong?"

"I saw him," Christina said, craning her head to see the field where she had seen a bay horse. "I swear, Mel, it was Speed.com. He was walking behind that little barn." She pointed at a small stable at the back edge of the property.

"Let's go check," Melanie said, putting the car in reverse.

"Let's call the police instead," Christina said, remembering what Dani had told her. "If it isn't him, we'd be trespassing, and if it is him, we'd be facing down a horse thief. Either way it isn't any good."

Melanie groaned. "You have no sense of adventure," she said, but she was smiling. "Okay, we'll call in the professionals as soon as we get back to the track."

When they arrived at Belmont, the girls went to the track office and found the security manager shuffling through papers. He glanced up when they walked in. "How can I help you?" he asked.

"We found Speed.com," Melanie blurted out.

The manager looked at her steadily. "Then you're the tenth person today who's found him," he said, shaking his head. "Give me the location and we'll have it checked out, but I doubt it's the missing horse."

Disappointed, they provided the information and left the office. "So much for being heroes," Melanie said dryly.

"We had a good time anyway," Christina countered.

Melanie tilted her head to the side and gazed at her cousin. "We did," she said. "Even without the Graham-Reese Detective Agency solving our first mystery."

"I think I'll stick to horse racing," Christina said. "Or veterinary college."

Melanie shot her a startled look. "Veterinary college?" she asked, grabbing at her chest. "Did I hear you say you're going to be a veterinarian?" She staggered, feigning a heart attack. "I can't believe my ears."

Christina shrugged. "That was a test," she said. "Now that I've seen your reaction, I won't tell anyone else until I've definitely made my decision."

"Good idea," Melanie said, then paused. "But I like it. I'd want you to work with my animals. You'd be a great vet, Chris."

"Thanks, Mel," Christina said, touched by her cousin's vote of confidence. They strolled toward the shed rows in companionable silence.

For the first time in weeks, Christina felt as though she and Melanie were reviving the friendship that had gotten them through so many years of living and working together. No matter what happened on Saturday, just the time she and Melanie were spending together made the trip to New York worthwhile.

9

THURSDAY MORNING CHRISTINA AND ASHLEIGH MET
Cindy, Melanie, Vince Jones, and Wild 'n' Free's jockey,
Justin Powers, at the track kitchen for breakfast.

"Has there been any word about Speed.com?" Ashleigh asked Vince as she sat down with her tray of
food.

Vince shook his head. "Not a peep," he replied.
"But even if they found him right away, the colt will
still be scratched from the race."

Christina took a bite of pancake and looked across
the table at Melanie. The horse they had seen the day
before must not have been Speed.com. Christina felt
disappointed that their tip to the security office hadn't
been a good one. After the excitement of thinking they

had seen the colt, she liked the idea of being part of recovering him for Dustin Gates.

Melanie took a drink of orange juice. "That means there'll be eight horses running on Saturday," she said. "That's a pretty small field for the Belmont."

Vince nodded. "It'll be easier on the horses that are running not to have a crowded field, but they're eight very good horses," he pointed out. "It's going to be quite a race."

"It'll be interesting to see how the draw for the gate positions plays out," Cindy commented, stabbing a sausage link with her fork. "With that small a field, I don't think there's a bad gate to come out of. It isn't like the horses will have a lot of traffic to deal with."

"Gate one is still the best spot," Ashleigh said. "Most of the Belmont winners have come out of the first chute."

"But gates three and five haven't done all that badly, either," Justin said. "I just hope Wild 'n' Free doesn't pull number eight. I don't think there's been a winner out of that spot."

"Yet," Cindy said quickly. "With a field this small, it's wide open."

After breakfast Christina and Ashleigh walked over to the racing secretary's office to join the group of trainers, jockeys' agents, and jockeys gathered there for the drawing of Saturday's races. The draw was scheduled for eleven o'clock, but even though they arrived in plenty of time, the office was already crowded.

Christina squeezed through the packed room and wedged herself between two other jockeys. She watched tensely as the secretary prepared to announce the starting positions for the races scheduled the day of the Belmont.

Most of the people in the room were there for the other races on the program. For each race, the secretary would give a spin to the tumbler full of numbered chips on the table in front of him. Then he would solemnly reach inside and withdraw a chip that would assign a gate number to one of the horses on his assistant's list.

Christina was always tempted to call out "Bingo!" after a race was drawn, but so far she had resisted the urge. The drawing for the Belmont was too serious for her to feel playful, so she watched intently as the track officials went through each of the races on the program. After the secretary called the draws for each race, the conversations between the agents, jockeys, and trainers grew louder for a few minutes, then settled down again as the next race's lineup was called, until finally they were down to the Belmont.

"We are drawing for the starting positions for the Belmont Stakes," the racing secretary's assistant said loudly, holding his clipboard and pen ready. The secretary gave the handle of the squirrel-cage tumbler a spin, and for a minute the only sound in the room was the soft whir as the tumbler full of chips spun around.

"TV Time," the assistant said. "Vicky Frontiere riding."

Christina held her breath as the secretary pulled a chip from the tumbler. "Gate seven," he announced.

"Magnifique," the assistant said, going to the next horse on his list.

"Gate two," the secretary said, reading the number on the chip.

Christina grimaced. Magnifique was getting an excellent starting position. But chute number one was still open. She crossed her fingers, hoping Star would be named in the first gate.

"Derry O'Dell," the assistant said.

"Three," the secretary announced.

"Wonder's Star."

Christina caught at her lip, waiting tensely to hear Star's gate number.

"Five," the secretary said.

Christina exhaled sharply. Gate five. Just like the

horrible dream she had when Star had gone down.

"War Ghost."

"Eight."

"Wild 'n' Free," the assistant read.

"Gate four," the secretary replied.

Christina swallowed at a lump that had started to form in her throat.

"Gratis."

"Gate number one."

"Yes!" Melanie's voice carried across the room.

Christina smiled to herself, glad that if Star wasn't getting the inside gate, at least Gratis and Melanie were getting a great starting position. But that left only gate six, and Celtic Mist would be the last horse on the list. A chill ran down Christina's back. Wild 'n' Free, Star, and Celtic Mist were positioned exactly as they had been in her nightmare.

She gave her head a quick shake. It was just a coincidence, she tried to tell herself. Star was going to be fine, and the race was going to go perfectly. The terrible nightmare had not been a premonition of how the Belmont was going to go.

As they left the racing secretary's office Melanie caught her arm. "You're going to be breaking right in the middle of the pack," she said. "That stinks."

Christina forced herself to smile. "That's the luck of the draw," she said, trying to shake the memory of her dream from her mind.

Ashleigh came out of the office with Vince Jones and Justin Powers. She walked over to Christina and Melanie while the other trainer and jockey walked on, talking about the race.

"Let's go figure out how we're going to handle the lineup," she told Christina, then smiled at Melanie. "Your job is pretty clear, isn't it?"

Melanie nodded. "All Gratis and I have to do is keep to the inside," she said. "It's going to be an exciting race."

"Yes, it will," Ashleigh said. "And I'm glad you're going to be riding in it, Mel."

"Me too," Melanie said. "Right now I'm supposed to meet Susan at the back lot. Since there isn't a lot to do this afternoon, she invited me to go shopping. We're both going to get new dresses for tomorrow night's prerace party at their apartment. And I'm kind of excited to do a mother-daughter thing with her, since we haven't had much time together."

Susan Graham had married Melanie's father after Melanie had moved to Whitebrook, so Melanie hadn't been around her stepmother much.

"I'll see you guys later," Melanie said as she headed for the parking lot.

Christina turned to her mother, tension gnawing at her stomach as she thought about the Belmont lineup. "How do you think I should work the field?" she asked.

Ashleigh looked grim. "You're flanked by two of the best horses in the field," she said. "I know the race is long, but if you're going to have a solid chance, you need to bring Star out at his top speed and keep him going right until the end. Most of the Belmont winners have set the pace and led the whole way." She paused. "Is it worth pushing him that hard?"

Christina bit at the inside of her cheek while she considered her mother's question, then exhaled heavily. "I would be cheating Star if we did any less," she finally said. "We'll come out and go for the front position right from the start. This is Star's last shot at one of the Triple Crown jewels. We need to put everything we have into it."

Ashleigh nodded in understanding. "If you want to play it differently, I won't be upset," she said.

"We're going to race to win," Christina told her mother. "You can count on it."

• • •

Early Friday afternoon Christina was sitting in front of Star's stall, cleaning tack. She went over her racing saddle carefully, making sure the lightweight vinyl was in perfect condition. When she was satisfied, checking the new girth she had attached to the off-billet, examining the stirrup leathers to make sure they were well oiled and strong, Christina leaned back for a moment and closed her eyes. She imagined herself on Star, waiting in the starting gate for the Belmont to start, and a shiver of anticipation coursed through her. *We need a perfect start*, she told herself. *We have to get out in front and stay there for the whole race.*

She felt a warm breath on her neck and tilted her chin back until she could see Star's long nose stretched down toward her. "We're going to have to make the cleanest break from the gate that racing history ever saw, boy," she said, reaching up to run her hand down his muzzle.

"Excuse us," a familiar voice called. "Is this the world-renowned Whitebrook stable?"

Christina popped her head up and stared in the direction of the voice. When she saw Derek and Elaine Griffen approaching Star's stall, she leaped to her feet. "Grandma, Grandpa!"

Derek Griffen extended his arms to sweep her into

a bear hug. "How's our favorite jockey?" he asked, stepping back to hold her at arm's length.

"You look wonderful, darling," Elaine Griffen said, pulling Christina away from her husband to give her a hug.

"I didn't know you were coming," Christina said, still shocked by the Griffens' appearance.

"What?" Her grandfather gave her a look of mock surprise. "We wouldn't have missed this for the world."

"Do Mom and Dad know you're here?" Christina demanded, giving her grandmother a kiss on the cheek.

Elaine shook her head. "We flew in from Arizona this morning," she said. "We had to do some finagling to get a motel room and tickets to the track, but we managed."

"We were going to wait until the prerace party tonight and surprise you," Derek said, looking at Christina's grandmother. "But Elaine couldn't stand waiting any longer to see you."

"This is so great," Christina said, her grin so wide that her face began to hurt.

"Star looks fantastic," Derek commented, stepping closer to the stall so that he could look closely at

Christina's colt. He glanced at Christina, a broad smile on his face. "He looks just like his dam," he said, running his hand along Star's jaw. "I still remember Wonder as a sickly little foal. No one thought she'd amount to anything, except your mother."

Elaine nodded in agreement. "And look at what you've done with Wonder's foal," she said. "It is going to be so much fun to watch you race, riding just like your mother did when she was your age."

"I understand Whitebrook and Tall Oaks are throwing quite a pre-Belmont party tonight at the Grahams'," Christina's grandfather said. "Really, we just came for the food, you know." He winked at Christina and gave her a broad smile.

"Derek!" Elaine Griffen exclaimed, shaking her head in dismay. "We came to watch Christina race."

"I'm so glad you're here, even if it's just for the shrimp cocktail," Christina told her grandfather. "Have you seen Mom yet? I think she's at the track office making sure all of our paperwork is in order."

"We'll work our way over there," Derek said, glancing around the shed row. "But I want to see some of the other horses."

"Me too," Elaine said, giving Christina another hug. "And we'll see you at the party tonight."

• • •

That evening Christina spent nearly an hour in Melanie's bedroom at Will and Susan Graham's. "Are you sure I look okay?" Christina asked her cousin, twisting to see her back in the full-length mirror. The sleeveless blue-and-white dress she wore had a short skirt that swirled a little every time she moved. She smoothed her hands down the skirt. "Maybe I should have brought a different outfit," she said.

"You look drop-dead gorgeous," Melanie replied, carefully stroking mascara onto her eyelashes. "It's too bad Parker won't be here to see you."

At the reminder, Christina's mood dropped a little. She hadn't heard from Parker since coming to New York. It was no surprise, with the schedule he was keeping, but still, she had thought he would let her know he was thinking of her.

"You know what?" Melanie asked, turning to look at Christina. "We may have missed our senior party, but I think this is going to be at least as much fun."

"I agree," Christina said. "I'm glad we're doing this, Mel."

"Me too," Melanie said. "And tomorrow, let's still be friends, okay? No matter how the race turns out."

Christina wrinkled her nose. "We've said that so many times that I don't know what to think anymore," she replied. "Let's just remember, no matter what, we're still related, so we have to get along, all right?"

Melanie burst into laughter. "You can pick your friends but you can't pick your family?"

"You've got it," Christina said.

Melanie crossed the room to give her a quick hug. "I would pick you as a friend even if you weren't my cousin," she said. "Even when we're mad at each other, I still love you, cuz."

When Christina and Melanie left the bedroom, several people were already gathered in the Grahams' spacious living room. The caterer had set up long tables along one wall, and each one was covered with trays of canapés. Christina stared at a tall figure reaching for a stuffed mushroom.

"Parker!" she exclaimed, stunned to see him.

When Parker turned to face her, he was smiling. "I wanted to surprise you," he said. "So, surprise. I'm here to watch you and Star race tomorrow."

"Thanks," Christina said, delighted. "I'm so glad you came up."

"It's really important for me to see you and Star run," Parker said. "And my mind won't be on eventing until the Belmont is run, anyway. Not with my favorite jockey riding." His quick grin looked almost embarrassed. Then he reached out to squeeze Christina's hand and looked deeply into her eyes. "Chris," he said, "I know we agreed that with our schedules, not trying to be a couple would be for the best, but I miss you a lot."

"I've missed you, too," she admitted. "I'm really glad you're here, Parker."

She saw Jazz crossing the room to give Melanie a hug, and noticed Will and Susan talking with Del Abdullah and Ghyllian Hollis.

When she caught sight of a couple talking to her mother, she gasped. "Jilly Gordon and Craig Avery," she exclaimed. "This is so cool." Jilly had jockeyed Ashleigh's Wonder until a broken leg kept her from racing, forcing Ashleigh to get her jockey's license so that she could ride Wonder in the Breeder's Cup.

Christina and Parker worked their way through the people in the room, ending up in the middle of a conversation with Ghyllian Hollis and Tor Nelson about Irish Thoroughbreds. Tor and Samantha had spent several years in Ireland and had met Ghyllian's father at the track.

Christina was distracted by what Tor was saying when she heard a phone ring in the distance.

A maid stepped into the room and gestured to Will, who followed her, only to return a minute later, looking excited. He caught Ashleigh by the elbow, leaning close to whisper something in her ear, and Christina tensed, afraid something was wrong with Star.

But when Ashleigh's eyes widened and her mouth popped open into a shocked O, Christina relaxed, sure that the message had nothing to do with her Thoroughbred colt.

She watched Ashleigh gesture to Cindy, who hurried to her side, and for a few minutes they whispered back and forth. Christina watched curiously, aching to know what was going on.

Finally Will waved his arms in the air. "Could I have everyone's attention for a minute?" he said loudly. "We just got an interesting piece of news."

The clusters of guests turned to look at Will, Ashleigh, and Cindy, waiting for Will to continue.

"Speed.com was just recovered," he said.

"Where was he?" Melanie asked, eyeing Christina.

"He was being kept at a small farm outside Elmont," Will told his daughter. "An anonymous tip led investigators to the location."

Christina and Melanie turned to look at each other, and Melanie gave an indifferent shrug. "At least they found him and he's all right," she said.

"Did they catch the thief?" Ben al-Rihani asked from where he was standing with Vince Jones.

"The investigation brought responsibility for his

disappearance back to his trainer, Alexis Huffman," Will said.

Christina turned to look at Melanie, who gave her a knowing smile and a nod. "We were right," Melanie mouthed to her.

"Interestingly enough," Will continued, "the vet who examined Speed.com upon his return to Belmont discovered that the colt has a hairline fracture in one cannon bone. If he had run tomorrow, he no doubt would have broken down before he could finish the race."

The room erupted into an energetic discussion of Alexis's theft of her own horse.

Once the excitement over Speed.com had settled down, Christina spent most of her time talking with Parker.

"I've thought about what you said about checking out the University of Kentucky campus," she said.

Parker grinned. "As soon as you get home, give me a call and I'll show you around the grounds," he said.

"But what about getting back to England?" Christina asked.

Parker smiled warmly at her. "Jack Dalton can wait a little while longer," he said.

"Okay," Christina said, gazing up at him. "I expect a great tour of the campus next week."

"You're on," Parker replied.

As the evening wore on, she found herself fighting to stay awake. Finally Ashleigh came over and touched her arm. "I think it's past your bedtime," she said.

Christina nodded. "I think you're right," she said. After wishing everyone a good night, they headed back to their motel, and Christina crawled into bed, worn out from the pre-Belmont excitement and tense over the next day's race. Over and over again her mind ran through the way she and Star would come out of the gate, until finally she drifted off to sleep, still fighting to keep the nightmare of Star breaking down out of the gate from slipping into her dreams.

10

"DUSTIN GATES IS PRESSING CHARGES AGAINST ALEXIS,"
Cindy said, when she stopped by Star's stall Saturday
morning. Christina and Dani had Star out of his stall,
grooming the colt for the race. Christina was running a
polishing brush along Star's already gleaming flank,
and she paused to look at Cindy.

"What will happen to her?" she asked.

Cindy wrinkled her nose. "The Thoroughbred racing association has already banned her from training
at any of the Thoroughbred tracks," she said. "I don't
know what else they'll do."

"But she could still get into one of the other horse-
racing circuits, right?" Dani commented, pulling a
comb through Star's shiny tail.

Cindy nodded. "If anyone will hire her," she said. "Alexis is obviously a survivor. She'll manage to get in with someone who doesn't know any better." She glanced across the aisle, where two grooms were preparing Celtic Mist for the race. "I need to get back to see how Beckie and Del's groom are doing with Gratis and Magnifique," she said.

As she walked away, Brad came down the aisle with a large group of people. He cast a cool look toward Star and Christina, then turned to his followers.

"Isn't that Wonder's Star?" someone asked.

Brad eyed Star and nodded. "Right now the odds on him are forty to one. He hasn't had very good showings in his last couple of races."

Christina stiffened. Forty to one? She caught Dani's eye. "No one believes in Star," she said.

"We do," Dani said firmly. "And no one knows him better than you. It's going to be a great race for him, Chris."

Christina exhaled, then gave Star's shoulder one last stroke with the brush. "I hope you're right," she said. "But forty to one? That's terrible."

"Other long shots have shown the oddsmakers how wrong they were," Dani retorted. "Star won't do any less. I predict a perfect race for him."

"It'll be great if you're right," Christina said. "Right

now I need to go weigh in. I'll see you and Star at the viewing paddock."

Melanie was coming out of the locker room as Christina walked into the jockeys' lounge. She crossed the room to greet the Tall Oaks jockey.

"I heard this is a record crowd for the running of the Belmont," a jockey commented, looking at Christina as he spoke. "I wish I were riding in that race."

Christina looked at her cousin and smiled thinly. "I have so many butterflies that it feels like they're running the Belmont in my stomach."

Melanie nodded in understanding. "We're both going to be fine," she said. "I'm sure of it."

That's easy for Melanie to say, Christina thought. *She and Gratis have the best starting position in the race.* Christina wished she could have the same confidence in herself and in Star. She knew that under the circumstances, she should be happy just to be racing her colt. But still, she felt a familiar competitive stirring that made her want to race to win.

After she dressed in her blue-and-white silks, she and Melanie carried their racing saddles to the scale for their official weigh-in.

When they returned to the main lounge several minutes later, the second race of the day was being run. They settled into chairs to watch the meet, tension shrouding both of them in silence.

Christina realized that in spite of Melanie's confident words, she was as nervous and worried about the race as Christina was. Christina remembered the awful moment in the Derby when Image had broken down, and the look of horror on Melanie's face as she had scrambled to get to the filly before she tried to stand on her broken leg.

Melanie had already gone through one of the worst things imaginable in a race, and Christina felt her edginess soften a little. She reached over and gave Melanie's arm a squeeze. "We are going to do great today," she said.

The smile Melanie offered her was clearly forced, but she nodded. "No matter what," she said in agreement.

When the time came to walk up to the viewing paddock, all of the jockeys were quiet. Christina could feel the tense energy humming in the air as the group approached the mounting area.

She saw Beckie holding Gratis, waiting for Melanie. The big bay colt tossed his head, trying to break free of his groom's hold, but Beckie kept him under control. Christina glanced at the saddle pad with it's big number one printed on the side, and she turned to her cousin.

"If Star and I don't beat the odds," she said, "I hope you and Gratis blow the rest of the field away."

Melanie gave her a grateful look. "Good luck, Chris," she said, then walked over to Beckie and Gratis.

Magnifique's jockey was already in the saddle as Christina walked on to where Dani was holding Star. She saw Tommy Turner getting a leg up onto War Ghost's back, and gave Vicky Frontiere a quick nod as Vicky spoke to TV Time's groom. Emilio Casados was murmuring something to Celtic Mist, his face close to the colt's gray nose, and Christina strode up to Dani, who gave her a confident nod.

"You'll rock," Dani said. "I know Star's going to be brilliant out there. Third time's the charm, Chris. This is Star's turn to shine."

"Thanks," Christina said, checking the girth before she let Dani boost her onto Star's back. She settled into place, and in a minute the grooms led the field of eight horses through the tunnel that led to the viewing area at the Belmont track, where her parents were waiting for her.

Christina sat easily on Star as they came into the packed grandstand area. She stared at the mass of people gathered near the rail, her attention settling on a group of familiar faces. Her grandparents were standing with Parker, Samantha and Tor, and Jilly and Craig.

When her grandfather caught her eye, he grinned broadly and gave her a thumbs-up, and Christina felt a little of her tension ease away. She and Star had their own special fan club. It didn't matter how the race came out; she had a lot of people who cared about her, which made her pretty lucky.

The stands were overflowing with racing fans, and as the field was led onto the track for the post parade, Christina leaned forward. "They didn't give you much of a chance with forty-to-one odds, Star. Let's shock them all, okay?"

Star pranced sideways, tugging at the lead line the pony rider held. When they turned back from their warm-up gallop to go into the gate, Star loaded eagerly, dancing in place with impatience. Christina patted his neck. "Save it, boy," she murmured. "We have a mile and a half to run. You're going to need all the energy you've got to pull this off."

In the chute beside her, Christina could hear Emilio muttering in Spanish to Celtic Mist. She heard the jangle of the bit as the colt tossed his head, while on her left she could hear Justin Powers talking to Wild 'n' Free, soothing the colt with his calm voice. She stared over the gate at the track stretching away in front of her, her eyes following the even lines of the furrows from the drag the track crew had used to smooth the dirt.

And as she waited to hear "One back!" before they loaded War Ghost, the horse in the number eight gate, a tense knot gripped her stomach with such force that she almost gasped in pain.

This is just like my nightmare. The thought echoed through her brain. *No!* she told herself. *This is real, and Star is going to do fine. We are going to run well, and we're going to finish up just fine.*

"One back!" was finally called, and Christina took a deep, steadying breath, collecting Star's reins as she positioned herself over his withers, prepared for the start.

When the gate snapped open, Star plunged onto the track. Christina felt the colt jolt forward as his hooves hit the dirt, and she sensed herself start to pitch onto his shoulders. "Oh, no!" she gasped, struggling to keep her balance. "This isn't happening."

But as Star surged forward, Christina realized the falling sensation had been her own fear. Star kept his feet, and they moved with the rest of the field toward the inside rail. She heaved a sigh of relief when she felt the colt strong and steady beneath her.

She quickly surveyed the horses running around her and saw Gratis and Celtic Mist in the lead.

"This is no good," she groaned. "We need to get up to the front right now," she told Star. But Vicky Frontiere had maneuvered TV Time up beside Star, and Wild 'n' Free was on the rail, running behind Gratis.

"Now what do we do?" Christina muttered, searching for a way to get Star into the clear. She could feel the colt fighting to speed up, but with nowhere to go, all the power he had wouldn't do them any good. Christina glanced under her arm to see Magnifique running strongly, but the big bay colt was caught behind the rest of the pack, and War Ghost was trailing behind.

"It's Gratis in the lead!" the announcer called, his voice ringing across the track. "It's Celtic Mist and Gratis side by side as they come into the first turn."

We're racing in the Belmont, Christina reminded herself, pressing her knuckles into Star's pumping neck. *That's all that matters. We've come this far, and that's good enough.* But she could feel in Star's strides, in the strain of his mouth against the bit, that the colt wanted to

155

win, and she knew he had it in him to do it—if they could just get out of the pack.

But as they moved along the backstretch she resigned herself to the fact that Star was not going to win the Belmont. And that was okay with her. "Don't strain yourself, boy," she told Star. "We'll run our best, but this isn't our race."

Star tugged at the reins, fighting her, but Christina held them firmly, keeping the colt in check. As they raced into the second turn, Gratis was still running strongly, neck and neck with Celtic Mist. Christina watched Melanie's hunched shoulders as she urged her colt on, her focus on the track ahead of her.

"It looks like it's going to be Gratis and Celtic Mist, wire to wire," the announcer called. "Wild 'n' Free is faltering, and Wonder's Star is holding strongly in fourth place."

But as they passed the marker for the eighth furlong, Wild 'n' Free dropped back. Christina started to urge Star to make a move, but before she could even shift her weight forward, Star dove for the hole the other colt left, tearing the reins from Christina.

Christina gasped and scrambled to keep Star under control. But Star was having none of it, and Christina remembered what Jean Cruguet, Seattle Slew's jockey, had said about racing Slew. *He just hung on and let the horse run the race his way,* she told herself. She relaxed her hands a little and leaned forward. "Do whatever you need to," she told her colt. Star snorted loudly and dug in, lengthening his strides as they drew near the lead horses.

"Wonder's Star is moving up! The forty-to-one long shot is making his move now! And he's going to do it! Look at this!" As though she were watching the race instead of riding it, Christina listened to the announcer describe Star's moves. She watched Gratis and Celtic Mist, their jockeys focused on each other as the two horses ran a speed duel, not sure that Star had enough time to pass the two powerful racehorses.

"Can we do this, boy?" she asked the colt. Star flicked his ears back and flew up behind them, blowing past the favored horses just as they crossed the finish line.

"It's Wonder's Star!" the announcer cried. "Wonder's Star has won the Belmont!"

As she began slowing her colt, the shocking realization of what had just happened swept over Christina. She and Star had just won the Belmont. She sat back in the saddle, turning Star, who seemed to think the race wasn't nearly over. As she brought the sweat-soaked colt to a stop, her mother and Dani ran onto the track to catch hold of him.

"You won!" Ashleigh exclaimed, throwing her arms around Christina as she jumped to the ground. "You won the Belmont!"

Christina gaped at her mother, still reeling over the race. "We couldn't have," she said. "Star broke badly, and he didn't take the lead from the start."

"You did it, you really did!" Dani said, circling Star as he snorted and blew, still dancing with excitement. "Let's get you to the winner's circle!"

As Christina followed Star back to the starting gate and the waiting throng at the winner's circle, she saw a tall dark-haired man standing near the rail, waving a bouquet of roses.

"You won!" Parker yelled, grinning broadly. Christina slowed as she reached him, and he leaned forward to thrust the flowers into her hands and press a quick kiss to her lips. "You and Star won!"

Christina nodded, still trying to absorb the reality. Star had really and truly won the Belmont. The roar of the crowd, the officials hustling her and Star into the winner's circle, Parker's joyful announcement—all made it real.

As she jumped back onto Star's back for the press photos and award ceremony, Christina patted Star's neck. "We made it, boy," she murmured. "You showed them all." Star tossed his head and snorted as a camera flashed, and for a few seconds the area around the winner's circle was busy with photographers getting pictures of the winner of the Belmont. Finally Star struck at the ground impatiently, and Ashleigh looked up at Christina.

"You've both had enough for now," she said, patting Christina's knee. "I think you have a special fan waiting for you." She nodded toward where Parker was waiting at the rail.

Christina caught Parker's eye as she slipped from Star's back, and the proud look on his face made her realize that he truly did care for her. In spite of all the odds against them, she and Parker were going to make it, too. And as she looked from Parker to the majestic racehorse that had risen to fame and success, she knew she was looking at her future, and everything was going to be just perfect.

SEATTLE SLEW
February 15, 1974–May 7, 2002

Seattle Slew was the first Triple Crown winner to be purchased at auction, for the price of $17,500. The bay Thoroughbred broke his maiden in his first race at Belmont, winning by five lengths, with a career race record of seventeen starts and fourteen wins. After nearly losing his jockey, Jean Cruguet, at the start of the 1977 Kentucky Derby, Slew recovered and won the race. Two weeks later in the Preakness, Seattle Slew ran the fastest opening mile in the race's history. After nearly dying of a viral infection at the age of four, he recovered and returned to the track to defeat Affirmed in the 1978 Marlboro Cup.

Mary Newhall Anderson spent her childhood exploring back roads and trails on horseback with her best friend. She now lives with her family and horses on Washington State's Olympic Peninsula. Mary has written novels and short stories for both adults and young adults.

WIN A FREE RIDING SADDLE!

ENTER THE
THOROUGHBRED RIDING SADDLE
SWEEPSTAKES!

COMPLETE THIS ENTRY FORM • NO PURCHASE NECESSARY

NAME: _____

ADDRESS: _____

CITY: _____ STATE: _____ ZIP: _____

PHONE: _____ AGE: _____

MAIL TO: THOROUGHBRED RIDING SADDLE SWEEPSTAKES!
c/o HarperCollins, Attn.: Department AW
10 E. 53rd Street   New York, NY 10022

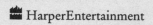 HarperEntertainment

17th Street Productions,
an Alloy Online, Inc., company

THOROUGHBRED 59 SWEEPSTAKES RULES

OFFICIAL RULES

1. No purchase necessary.

2. To enter, complete the official entry form or hand print your name, address, and phone number along with the words "Thoroughbred Riding Saddle Sweepstakes" on a 3" x 5" card and mail to: HarperCollins, Attn.: Department AW, 10 E. 53rd Street, New York, NY 10022. Entries must be received by October 1, 2003. Enter as often as you wish, but each entry must be mailed separately. One entry per envelope. Partially completed, illegible, or mechanically reproduced entries will not be accepted. Sponsors are not responsible for lost, late, mutilated, illegible, stolen, postage due, incomplete, or misdirected entries. All entries become the property of HarperCollins and will not be returned.

3. Sweepstakes open to all legal residents of the United States (excluding residents of Colorado and Rhode Island) who are between the ages of eight and

sixteen by October 1, 2003, excluding employees and immediate family members of HarperCollins, Alloy, Inc., or 17th Street Productions, an Alloy company, and their respective subsidiaries, and affiliates, officers, directors, shareholders, employees, agents, attorneys, and other representatives (individually and collectively), and their respective parent companies, affiliates, subsidiaries, advertising, promotion and fulfillments agencies, and the persons with whom each of the above are domiciled. Offer void where prohibited or restricted.

4. Odds of winning depend on total number of entries received. Approximately 100,000 entry forms distributed. All prizes will be awarded. Winners will be randomly drawn on or about October 15, 2003, by representatives of Harper-Collins, whose decisions are final. Potential winners will be notified by mail and a parent or guardian of the potential winner will be required to sign and return an affadavit of eligibility and release of liability within 14 days of notification. Failure to return affadavit within the specified time period will disqualify winner and another winner will be chosen. By acceptance of prize, winner consents to the use of his or her name, photographs, likeness, and personal information by HarperCollins, Alloy, Inc., and 17th Street Productions, an Alloy company, for publicity and advertising purposes without further compensation except where prohibited.

5. One (1) Grand Prize Winner will receive a Thoroughbred riding saddle. HarperCollins reserves the right at its sole discretion to substitute another prize of equal or of greater value in the event prize is unavailable. Approximate retail value $500.00.

6. Only one prize will be awarded per individual, family, or household. Prizes are nontransferable and cannot be sold or redeemed for cash. No cash substitute is available except at the sole discretion of HarperCollins for reasons of prize unavailability. Any federal, state, or local taxes are the responsibility of the winner.

7. Additional terms: By participating, entrants agree a) to the official rules and decisions of the judges which will be final in all respects; and b) to release, discharge, and hold harmless HarperCollins, Alloy Online, Inc., and 17th Street Productions, an Alloy Online, Inc., company, and their affiliates, subsidiaries, and advertising promotion agencies from and against any and all liability or damages associated with acceptance, use, or misuse of any prize received in this sweepstakes.

8. To obtain the name of the winner, please send your request and a self-addressed stamped envelope (Vermont residents may omit return postage) to "Thoroughbred Riding Saddle Winners List," c/o HarperCollins, Attn.: Department AW, 10 E. 53rd Street, New York, NY 10022.

SPONSOR: HarperCollins*Publishers* Inc.